OUT ON A LIMB

By Carolyn Jourdan

In this book Smoky Mountain dialect is rendered as it sounds. Appalachian speech is poetic and musical. It's sung as much as spoken, so a significant portion of the meaning is conveyed in the cadences and tones.

Dialect is used in conversation by people of all levels of education and intelligence, so no apostrophes will highlight dropped g's or word variants, as if they are errors. For the same reason, the local grammar is retained, as are phrases in dialect such as "in the floor" instead of "on the floor."

This was done to enable the reader to experience Smoky Mountain life and language intimately, as an insider would.

This is a work of fiction.
For safety reasons, locations and routes described herein have been intentionally altered to preclude retracing.

E-Book ISBN – 13: 978-0-9885643-3-6
Printed Book ISBN – 13: 978-0-9899304-5-1
Printed in the United States of America

Designed by Karen Key

Cover photograph by Donna Eaton
deatonphoto@gmail.com
www.donnaeatonphoto.com

CHAPTER 1

Ivy Iverson knew what she was doing was extremely dangerous. She'd been warned time and again by her friends and family. They'd cautioned her about going out into the wilderness alone, and making these high ascents alone. They'd begged her to at least tell someone where she was going.

But she preferred to do things her own way.

She was going *way* out on a limb, and she loved the feeling more than anything in the world. She stood over a hundred feet high on a branch near the top of a leviathan hemlock in the Great Smoky Mountains National Park.

It was sunrise and patches of white mist slowly rolled by as she reconfigured her climbing gear. She stopped to watch the surreal mist creep through the upper branches of the old-growth tree, each wisp looking like a ghostly form fleeing the rising sun. The chill of the early morning damp caused a shiver to race down her spine.

Shrugging off the cold, she clipped on a temporary safety line, hauled up the long dangling ropes she'd used to get where she was, and prepared for the next segment of her ascent. A climb this high had to be done in stages or else the rope would be too heavy for her to handle. She scanned the canopy until she saw another limb about fifty feet overhead that looked sturdy enough to bear her weight, and then braced herself against the tree trunk while she reloaded her crossbow.

When she was ready, she took a couple of deep breaths, turned around, and paced carefully backwards along the swaying limb. She moved gracefully, like an acrobat on a high wire. When she got a clear shot, she stopped and balanced herself as well as possible.

Holding the crossbow snug against her right shoulder, she fired a perfect shot. The bolt, trailing lightweight cord in its wake, soared over the limb and dropped onto the other side, falling neatly in front of her.

Ivy tied the thin cord to the end of her orange and yellow climbing rope and teased and tugged until the climbing rope had replaced it across the limb above her. This would be the final segment of the climb, so she wouldn't need the crossbow again this morning. She used the long cord to lower it to the ground. When it touched down gently next to her backpack, she let go of the cord and it fell so it lay with the rest of her gear at the base of the tree. With the ease of long practice, she re-rigged her harness and connected it to the climbing ropes.

Then she checked the exotic knot on which her life depended. It was a Blake's hitch, a knot commonly used by arborists to climb trees. The knot could slide upwards easily, but wouldn't allow any downward travel unless it was held in a particular way with continuous pressure. When she was satisfied that all her gear was configured correctly, she began to climb again.

Her shoulders were unusually muscular for a woman. They'd been honed by working out six days a week and climbing trees in all her free time, so it didn't take her long to reach her goal. Her formidable expertise in scaling trees had earned her the nickname Ivy.

When she reached the limit of her rope there were no big limbs nearby to stand or sit on, so she remained seated in her harness, swinging. She took in the view while she got her breath back. She was in the higher elevations of the Smokies at over 5,000 feet, plus the 150 more she'd just climbed, amid an incredibly lush and diverse forest that was an International Biosphere Reserve.

She was off-trail in a remote area of the park that could be identified only by GPS coordinates. But this was typical for her. Most of the really big trees were hard to get to, or they would never have escaped the greedy saws of loggers in the early 1900's.

The climbing made her hot, so she unzipped her jacket and took off her helmet. She ran a hand through her sweaty sun-streaked blond hair, then clipped the helmet to her harness while she enjoyed her surroundings. Her shoulder muscles were burning from exertion and her hands chafed inside her gloves.

She was in paradise. Her vantage point was atop a thick blanket of clouds that totally concealed the undulations of the blue-green ridges below her. The only part of the Appalachians she could see were the tips of the tallest peaks. They looked like islands rising above a turbulent white sea.

The sunrise was casting a pink, gold, and orange glow onto the ever-present, ever-changing, clouds and fog that gave the Smoky Mountains their name. It was a perfect time of year to be in the park. When the cloud cover burned off she'd be able to enjoy one of the early fall days when the mountainside reflected three seasons simultaneously: lush green of summer at the lowest elevations, gaudy fall color in the middle, and austere bare branches of winter on the mountaintops.

It was almost too beautiful to bear. The peace of the vast forested wilderness was complete. The only sounds were made by birds and leaves rustling in the breeze.

Now that she'd stopped exerting herself, she became aware of the pervasive dampness and the places her harness was cutting into her legs. The best way to ease the pain and restore circulation was to carefully rotate her body until she was hanging upside-down with her feet pointed toward the sky. A couple of minutes like that were all she needed and all her heart could tolerate, but it really helped refresh her.

As she upended herself several birds burst into flight as though startled by something nearby. Ivy squinted, wondering if a bear might be making its way along the forest floor. A bear was the only creature in the Smokies that could present a serious threat to a person in a tree.

It was rare for a bear to eat meat. They preferred a vegetable diet, but they were called *opportunistic eaters*. In certain circumstances they could turn predatory to other animals and even humans.

She'd seen the jumbled piles of bare, crushed bone fragments left from a bear kill and the bear scat with bits of bone in it. She thought of them as *bear bones* even though they were anything but that.

Peering down through the layers of branches, she caught sight of something large lumbering in her direction. The critter, whatever it was, raised up on its hind legs, and she caught her breath.

It wasn't a bear, it was a man.

Someone stood below her with his head tilted back, staring straight toward her as she swung upside-down in her harness. That was odd. Ivy hadn't told anyone where she was going this morning. But now, someone was staring at her from behind a ski mask and it wasn't really cold enough to warrant one.

Blood was rushing to her head and her heart was pounding from being upside-down. She suddenly felt nauseous.

"Hello?" she called out, hoping for a friendly reply.

The mysterious hiker remained silent and turned his attention to something he was holding. Whoever he was, his intentions were not benign, for Ivy realized with a shiver that he was holding her crossbow. Then he lifted it and aimed it squarely at her.

CHAPTER 2

Phoebe McFarland exhaled and watched the plume of her breath fade slowly in the cold morning air. She stood alone on a ridge in the pre-dawn darkness, facing a landscape that was corrugated like a washboard. At this early hour the twilight panorama was the color of tarnished silver and pencil lead.

The Smokies always looked so peaceful. But Phoebe knew it was dangerous to underestimate what you were looking at. Beauty could be used as bait for something unpleasant, while treasures were often concealed behind the plainest of façades. Some people figured this out early, others stayed foolish about it their whole lives.

She had a hard day to get through and didn't know how she was going to make it. Sean's funeral was at noon. His sudden death three days ago had been a hard blow to Phoebe. She wasn't yet used to the idea that he was gone.

Phoebe had never married. Sean was the latest in a long string of boyfriends that stretched back nearly forty years. He would be the last, Phoebe thought. This clinched it. No more men, even good ones like Sean.

As the night reluctantly yielded to the dawn, tints of inky blue and evergreen were revealed. The view was sublime. With no cars, houses, or manmade objects of any kind in sight, or in earshot, there was just the dawn and the marvelously varied greens and blues of the Smoky Mountains stretched out before her, easing her heart as she knew it would.

She was grateful that no matter what else was going on in her life, she always had these beautiful, lumpy old mountains for solace. They were the one constant in her chaotic world. She knew the Smokies hadn't always looked this way. Geologists claimed that millions of years ago they'd been higher than the Himalayas after being thrust up from an ocean bed in an immense collision of the super continent Pangaea.

For eons afterwards, towering walls of rock more than five miles high had weathered down to nubs. Then they'd been teased up high again when Africa crashed against North America before the continents settled into the places they currently occupied. These days, the hunchback ridges were thought to be in their third decline, brought low by two hundred and fifty million years of erosion.

That was the cycle of life, Phoebe thought, youthful exuberance meeting wear and tear. Standing up and getting knocked down, over and over again. The ancient mountains presented a deceptively soft and gentle appearance. Just like a lot of people as they aged. But looks could be deceiving, whether it was people or landscapes.

In fact, looks were nearly always deceiving in one way or another, Phoebe mused. This was especially so in the southern Appalachian highlands. Outsiders tended to see whatever they wanted to see, *The Beverly Hillbillies, Deliverance,* or *Mayberry.* In truth, this was home to a vastly underestimated and misunderstood people. If a medical analogy could be made, the regional culture would be called a *syndrome,* a cluster of odd symptoms that might seem unrelated unless you were smart enough to correctly identify what you were looking at.

In this case, the distinctive constellation of characteristics were that the inhabitants were tough as boot leather, wildly emotional on the inside while struggling to appear stoic on the outside, deeply spiritual, and possessed with an irrepressible, zany sense of humor. Phoebe had been born and raised here, so she was one of them, but she'd spent many years living in large cities like Miami and Washington as an adult, so she had some insight into how the local eccentricities were viewed by the rest of the world.

She'd driven up to Poplar Ridge before starting her workday because it was the place she liked to come when she was troubled. The view from there never failed to work on her like a tonic. Of course, one person's medicine was another person's poison. Phoebe wasn't sure what made her think of that ancient warning, but she whispered the Latin phrase like an incantation to ward off evil, *Quod medicina aliis, aliis est acre venenum.*

Phoebe was familiar with death, she was a nurse after all. But Sean's death had been so mysterious. He'd died on a hiking trail from a head wound. The coroner's best guess was that he'd slipped and fallen and hit his head on a rock.

But Sean didn't hike. He liked to fish, but Phoebe had never known him to go hiking. It was unsettling. She wondered if outsiders were right and these mountains were somehow ominous. Maybe the smoke concealed evil, or a powerful kind of bad luck.

Well, even if it'd been a mistake to come back to East Tennessee, what was done, was done. She stood shivering in the cold, lingering for a few more minutes until the sun finally burst above the mountains in a glorious flare of gold and pink. That was what she'd been waiting for. Phoebe let the solar fire burn her eyes until she felt able to get on with her life. It was amazing how a bit of warmth and light was often all a person needed.

She made her way back to her car. Now that the sun was up, she could see the last of the tall summer wildflowers rising out of a ground-hugging mist, brilliant yellow goldenrod and deep purple ironweed. A knobby-kneed elk with an oversize set of antlers stepped out of the woods and looked around. He reminded Phoebe of a showgirl trying to prance around gracefully while wearing a preposterous headdress. He looked toward her and sniffed the air, his breath creating clouds of condensed water vapor around his head.

She got into her Jeep, a little hospital on wheels that served her faithfully as she ran the mountain roads on her rounds as a home health care nurse. As she drove away, calmed by the apparent serenity of the wilderness, she didn't realize another cataclysmic collision was taking place deep in the forest. Not a prehistoric collision of continents this time, but a violent collision between two people.

CHAPTER 3

The attacker had been waiting patiently for just this moment, for the girl to remove her helmet and invert herself. It presented a clear shot at her head.

Ivy barely had time to register the enormity of the situation before the first arrow hit her. But even if she'd seen it coming, hanging upside-down, she had little chance to avoid the blow since there was nothing to hide behind, or to kick against, to propel herself out of the way.

The bolt hit her in the right thigh and the shock of the impact made her drop her legs so she was jerked upright. Luckily she was at the extreme range of the crossbow and her bolt had a padded, practice tip. A sharp hunting point was far too dangerous to use as a rope launcher. Still, the arrow hit her with the force of a hammer, sending pain jangling up and down her right side, and set her spinning wildly.

She knew she'd be safer if she could climb higher, or get on top of a big limb, but she'd never make it onto the branch she was dangling underneath. She was hurt and in pain. There'd be too much scrambling involved to climb onto it from her position. She could descend and swing over onto a limb below her, but that would send her closer to her assailant. No, she decided she'd try to move around to the other side of the tree trunk, like squirrels did when they were being chased.

As Ivy swung, she flailed her arms and legs, trying to grab hold of something, anything, that would help her control her trajectory, but the small tips of branches she was able to reach tore off in her hands, and panic bloomed in her mind at the very real possibility she might die out here far away from any help, totally alone.

No, no, no, she thought. Ivy kicked to widen her swing, hoping she was making a more difficult target, but it felt like precious little protection when she saw her attacker had retrieved the arrow and was reloading the crossbow.

When the weapon tilted up toward her again, she lifted her legs and put her face to her knees in an inverted jackknife that presented her butt as the biggest target. That would shield her as well as possible.

The second shot slammed into her back, at the top of her left hip. The savage blow forced her to let go of the rope and drop her legs again. The lower half of her body was paralyzed with pain.

She hung, limp as a ragdoll, helpless to save herself, and watched the dark figure reel in the cord for another shot.

"Stop!" she shouted, "I'll do whatever you want. Please stop!"

There was nothing she could do to evade the third shot. The bolt slammed into the side of her head with enough force to penetrate her skull had it been carrying a metal tip. As it was, the impact of the arrow was hard enough to knock her unconscious. Her body flopped into a boneless backbend, swinging and spinning.

Ivy would have fallen out of the tree if the Blake's hitch hadn't fulfilled its function as dead man's switch and held her aloft. Even if she'd been conscious, though, her erratic movements and upside-down perspective would've made it impossible for her to follow the movements of her attacker, let alone defend herself.

Luckily, her body's gyrations made it equally difficult for the shooter to notice what was happening, preoccupied as he was with reloading the crossbow. Ivy's slumped posture and rotation had upended the canvas equipment pouch that was clipped to the waistband of her harness and was spewing its contents. Announced by only a faint metallic jingle and zing, a hail of shrapnel made of spare carabiners, pliers, a buck knife, a folding saw, and a small hammer plummeted fifteen stories in a brutal metal rain.

Even the most mundane object could become deadly when dropped from a hundred and fifty feet. The folding saw tore a gash in her attacker's scalp, while the pliers, and buck knife cut and bruised his face and shoulder. The slender bolt took a direct hit from the hammer and snapped in two, making the crossbow useless.

Her assailant was stunned by the blows to his head and fell to his knees. With a broken arrow and no rope, he had no way to reach Ivy. He had no means to inflict further harm on her. The lowest limb of the hemlock and the trailing end of her rope were more than eighty feet off the ground. Nobody could get to her now without a lot of climbing gear.

Enraged, he removed the broken pieces of the arrow and tossed them away. Then he crawled to the base of a tree a few yards away, slumped against the trunk, and tended to his wounds as best he could, wary of anything else that might fall.

Ivy's body danced high overhead, gradually losing momentum in its swing and spin. Her attacker waited and watched for a long time, alert for the slightest indication that she might still be alive.

He was mightily frustrated not to be able to retrieve her body, but the more he thought about it, the more confident he became that it would never be found. The park was huge and the terrain was extremely rugged. Fortunately for him Ivy had a habit of going out alone wherever her whims took her and not telling the Park Service or anyone else where she was headed or when she'd be back.

She was well off any trail and hidden among the tree canopy. Even when the leaves were gone, it was unlikely she'd ever be spotted. Off-trail hikers didn't look up while they walked. They kept their eyes on the ground because of the treacherous terrain and the very real possibility of poisonous snakes.

The encounter hadn't gone the way he'd planned. He'd set out intending to talk to her, or at worst threaten her. But then he'd seen her lower the crossbow to the ground.

It was impulsive to use it, but the improvisation saved him a lot of wrangling. He pondered the situation and realized it was a perfect crime.

The wind blew, leaves rustled, and the rope creaked softly as Ivy swayed. Finally, satisfied that if she wasn't already dead, she soon would be, the attacker gathered up her gear and purple backpack and walked away, leaving her hanging there like a circus performer frozen in mid-act, forever stranded between heaven and earth.

CHAPTER 4

Blissful ignorance was great while it lasted, but if you had any brains at all it was impossible to remain clueless forever. Phoebe knew everybody went through rough patches, but this had gone too far. Nothing in her life was working out like she'd pictured.

Early in her career she'd wanted to experience the wider world beyond the Smoky Mountains, so she'd moved away. She'd been shocked to find herself in places where people didn't want to know, much less care about, their neighbors. For years she'd made good money as a nurse and worked her way up the ladder. But it bothered her to see affluent and cultured people congregating in picturesque enclaves from which they displayed the same haughty disinterest in their neighbors as they did the beggars sleeping on grates less than a block away.

That was no life for Phoebe. She loved people, all kinds of people. A person with her open and friendly ways couldn't bear to live her whole life in a disconnected urban environment. So, six months ago, when she'd heard that the local doctor needed to retire and no one was willing to take his place, she'd ditched her career, moved back home to White Oak, Tennessee, and taken a job with the beleaguered rural health care agency that served the area. A good home health care nurse could take up a lot of the slack in a community that lost its doctor.

Finally she was back where she'd grown up, where she knew everyone and they knew her. But in all her imaginings of what it would be like to return to the quirky mountain community she'd been raised in, she'd never envisioned this particular scenario.

When it should've been impossible for her day to get worse, it had gotten much, *much* worse. Instead of being on the road to Sean's funeral, she was cowering in a bathroom at the Talley's home trying to escape Wanda Talley, the diabetic from hell.

A couple of minutes earlier Wanda had abruptly stopped screaming threats and pounding on the door and shuffled away in the distinctive gait of a person with peripheral neuropathy. Now she was back and eerily silent. Phoebe could hear her breathing heavily on the other side of the door and making metallic scratching noises near the knob.

Wanda was a 375-pound housebound diabetic who was out of control in more ways than one. When Phoebe had tested her that morning, Wanda's blood sugar was sky-high and she complained that she'd lost all the feeling in her feet. Wanda had gone from being able to regulate her disease with pills to needing multiple insulin injections every day.

Phoebe hated to stand by and watch someone eat herself into an early grave. So she decided to take extreme measures to save Wanda's life. She made a sweep of the premises and discovered a stash of doughnuts under the bed as well as half a bag of Double Stuff Oreos. Then she found a family-size pack of Peanut M&Ms hidden behind a roll of toilet paper underneath the bathroom sink. She'd seized the forbidden items and naively attempted to walk out the front door with them. But Phoebe failed to anticipate the magnitude of Wanda's sugar addiction and thus the violence of her reaction to the confiscation of her guilty pleasures.

In a matter of seconds Phoebe was suddenly, and quite unexpectedly, running for her life. But that brought her only as far as the bathroom. Now she was trapped in there with the carbs.

Phoebe was genuinely concerned for Wanda. She had to find a way to help her get control of her diet and lose weight. If not, Wanda's diabetes was going to land her in the middle of a dirt sandwich. And soon.

"Wanda," she said, loud enough to be heard on the other side of the door, "have you ever tried tapping?"

There was no response aside from an increased intensity in the scraping at the lock.

"It's an alternative type of therapy that works well for a lot of people. It's sorta like acupressure-meets-psychotherapy. It's free, you can do it yourself, you don't need any equipment, and there's no drugs involved. Why don't we give it a try?"

Phoebe waited, but Wanda's persistent scratching continued.

She soldiered on, gamely, "In tapping, you try to discover whatever's really botherin you, the thing that's makin you overeat in the first place. You tap on a series of acupressure spots and say things like, 'Even though I eat too much, I totally love and unconditionally accept myself.'"

Again, Wanda said nothing.

"The idea comes from the Carl Rogers School of psychotherapy, you know, the unconditional positive regard fellow? This is a kind of do-it-yourself version of his thing, plus clearing the Chinese energy meridians at the same time."

The only reply was Wanda's ongoing lock picking efforts.

"Let's tap on ourselves, okay?" Phoebe said, trying to sound brave, knowing full well that Wanda intended do a lot more than *tap* on her when she got through the door.

"First you tap on the center of your eyebrow with the middle finger of your dominant hand."

Phoebe went through the first couple of steps of the tapping process, alone. Then she gave up. She needed to try something else. "Okay, forget tapping. There's lots of different approaches that work, like meditation and centering prayer. Those techniques can be really effective, too. The training for Trappist monks, the ones who don't talk, is very similar to the 12 Steps. Did you know that?"

Obviously Wanda had a pretty strong ability to maintain focus, but unfortunately it was on sugar instead of the Lord or world peace. Phoebe looked around for an exit. The window was the only possibility. She briefly considered trying to flush the armload of junk food she'd confiscated, but didn't want to clog up the toilet.

Wanda needed some time to climb down from her sugar high and cool off. And Phoebe needed to get away.

She unlocked the window and heaved up on the bottom sash. It shuddered slowly upward. She clicked the little latches on the screen and moved it out of the way, too. She was scooping up the contraband she'd dumped onto the vanity when Wanda succeeded in picking the lock and burst through the door ready to wreak havoc.

Phoebe dropped the sweets and lunged awkwardly out the window.

Fortunately it was only three feet off the ground. She regained her footing and made a mad dash for her Jeep, ripped the door open, flung herself inside, and raced away in a hail of flying gravel without looking back.

There were some people in this world that you couldn't reason with.

CHAPTER 5

The Great Smoky Mountains National Park was the most popular national park in the country. It was visited by nine million people a year, twice as many as went to the Grand Canyon and three times as many as toured Yosemite.

But because the Smokies was mostly a steep, trackless wilderness bisected by a single road, and because people generally didn't wander more than fifty yards from their cars, the park was experienced by most tourists as a gigantic drive-thru forest. The place was filled with vegetation so lush, if there actually was a place on earth where you couldn't see the forest for the trees, this would be it.

It was probably a good thing that the millions of people didn't venture very far out into the woods. What looked pretty from the car could easily turn into a death trap to the unwary or unprepared. The propensity of outsiders to underestimate the park was highlighted by the world's most famous travel writer, Bill Bryson, in his bestselling book *A Walk in the Woods*. Bryson set out to hike the 2,174 mile Appalachian Trail and started at the southern terminus in Georgia, walking north. But shortly after entering the 72-mile stretch of trail that passes through the Great Smoky Mountains National Park, he changed his mind and abandoned his plan.

Even a modest taste of the park forced a world-renowned

professional traveler to give up his dream, call for a cab, and flee to the nearest airport. Every day all sorts of adventures were begun, or ended, in the nation's most beloved patch of woods.

In the span of a single day, the park might host events covering the entire span of a human life – birth, birthday party, romantic liaison, engagement, wedding, honeymoon, vacation, anniversary, reunion, accident, injury, illness, death, funeral, and burial. A vast array of activities took place year round, some accidental, some intentional, some legal, some not.

Several times a year a nonprofit research organization, Discover Life in America, known as DLIA, set up conferences for the All Taxa Bio-Inventory project in the Smokies. During these gatherings, dozens of scientists with expertise in biology and botany congregated in the national park for a few days to survey designated plant, animal, and insect species. Each scientist led a gang of volunteers, referred to as *Citizen Scientists*, who combed over selected areas of the park looking for the species chosen for study.

This week there were several DLIA surveys taking place simultaneously. Each of the teams needed volunteers, so the surveys were given enticing names like Fern Foray, Karst Quest, or Beetle, Butterfly, and Bat Blitzes.

Only three of the events were restricted to participants with special skills: the karst and bat surveys and the search for leviathan trees. All three of those required climbing and rappelling skills. The karst and bat work was done in caves. The tree searches were carried out in places so remote and arduous to traverse that only a few ultra-hardy and ultra-cocky souls ever attempted to participate.

In the search for the tallest trees, even among the experienced hikers who were the fittest people imaginable, most of them ended up bailing in shame after an hour or two of attempting to wade through rhododendron and mountain laurel thickets. The extreme sport of trying to move through the tangled shrubbery, called *hells* by the locals, was referred to as *rhodo surfing*. It was an activity that only a handful of people in the world enjoyed.

Most of the surveys took place within a yard or less of well-known hiking trails since off-trail hiking, or even walking more than ten feet off a well-trod path, in the Smoky Mountains was considered suicidal. A mountainous jungle was not a place you wanted to get lost in. So, for a few days a couple hundred people would crash around in the undergrowth, then go home sunburned, bug-bitten, slashed by briars, happy to have had a productive adventure in nature.

Luckily for Ivy's attacker, the scientists were focused very narrowly, so there wasn't much chance any of them would notice him or Ivy.

He'd been tracking Ivy's excursions for over a month, and he'd learned how to enter and leave the groves of old growth forest without becoming lost. There were a couple of hiking trails that swathed through the corridors of ancient trees, but the places Ivy was interested in were well away from those.

If you had basic orienteering skills there were techniques for maintaining your bearings in any wilderness setting. The main thing to know about the Greenbrier area of the park was that from the air, the topography looked like a hand with the fingers spread out. The fingers were the ridges and the spaces between them were the valleys. He could keep track of his position by counting the finger hollows he traversed.

With the help of a detailed topographical quad map from the U.S. Geological Service, he knew which streams branched off where, and which ones would eventually lead back to the road. It wasn't easy, but practice made perfect. After several expeditions, the trip had become routine.

This time, however, he needed to exercise extreme caution. It wouldn't do to be noticed in the area. Although he doubted Ivy would be found for a long time, if ever, it was conceivable that a hiker might stumble into the area. In winter, when the leaves were off, it was possible that someone might spot her, and then questions would be asked about who might've been seen in the area.

He needed to get away without being noticed and he needed to do whatever he could to make sure her body was never found. That meant he had to lay a false trail for searchers. He could use her backpack for that. Then he'd move her car.

People who knew Ivy knew how she loved to spend time in the park. He could use that to his advantage. He'd leave the backpack where it would be discovered, but it wouldn't be anywhere near Greenbrier. He'd take it to the far west side of the park and leave it in the busiest area, Cades Cove.

That way the search and rescue team would scour the wrong place. When her disappearance was noticed, there'd be a massive search, but after several days or a week of coming up empty-handed, the efforts would diminish. Ivy would become just another sad entry in the long list of people who'd vanished in the Smokies.

He neared the edge of the woods and the road a few hundred yards from his car. He stopped to listen for any vehicles coming. The only sounds he heard were of the wind sighing through the trees, birds calling, and air heaving in and out of his lungs. It hurt when he peeled off his ski mask. And he had to concentrate to take longer, deeper breaths to calm himself.

He touched his head gingerly where Ivy's folding saw had struck him. His hand came back smeared with blood. He felt the scrapes and bruises on his face and shoulder and his split lip. *She got what she deserved,* he thought.

Although he'd been toying with the idea of somehow getting rid of her, the fact that he'd actually done it was just now hitting home. He had killed a person. He'd terminated the earthly existence of a human being.

A weaker man might break down at this point or waver in his resolve. But he wasn't squeamish. Now that the deed was done, he found he wasn't a bit sorry. And he realized it would be easy to do it again if need be.

The thought was oddly freeing, then downright exhilarating. He'd crossed a line that put everything in a whole new context. He wadded up the ski mask and shoved it into his pocket. He waited until he was sure no cars were coming in either direction, then he stepped out onto the road.

CHAPTER 6

Leon Lowery was standing in the middle of the road looking like a character in a low-budget redneck horror movie when Phoebe clapped eyes on him. He appeared to have been gargling blood and then spit it up all over himself. He'd taken off his ragged t-shirt and was using it to wipe himself off, but his efforts weren't very effective. He was mostly just smearing the blood around.

Phoebe drove right up to where he was standing and got out. She took a quick look at his pale skin and tall bony frame draped in threadbare blue jeans and canvas tennis shoes with holes in them. He didn't seem to be hurt very bad. The blood was coming from a busted lip and a superficial laceration on his head.

"Leon, I swear," said Phoebe, with an encouraging smile and a comforting voice, "if it's not one thing, it's another."

She walked around to the back of her Jeep, opened the door, and rummaged around in her supplies. She opened a cooler, filled a baggie with ice cubes, and zipped it closed. Then she wrapped the homemade cold pack in a clean cotton towel and gave it to him. "Hold this against your mouth, honey. It'll keep the swelling down."

Leon mumbled thanks and placed the ice carefully against his swollen lip.

"Sit down before you fall down," she said, indicating he should sit on the edge of the cargo area. She removed his baseball cap and mirrored sunglasses and set them carefully to one side while she made a closer inventory of his injuries.

"What happened?" she asked.

"Wrecked," he mumbled. "Dog in the road."

Leon didn't like to waste words.

"Anybody else hurt?"

He shook his head. "Dog's fine."

"Well," said Phoebe, "that's good. Now close your eyes."

She dabbed gently at the blood on his face and neck and hands until she had him cleaned up, then she disinfected his wounds the best she could. Fortunately, he didn't need any stitches. As Phoebe began to pack up her gear, he slipped his sunglasses and hat back on and, in iconic redneck style, lit a cigarette. That was Leon, smoking with a split lip that had to hurt like the dickens.

Phoebe guessed it was part of his artistic lifestyle. He was a bluegrass musician. He could play anything. Even as a kid he'd been able to sing and clog like a professional.

Nobody had been surprised when he'd moved to Nashville. He'd made a good living as a studio musician and eventually been offered his own record deal, and that didn't surprise anybody either. But one day something happened to him, and he walked away from it all. From the money, the fame, everything.

There were widely differing accounts of what had happened, but everyone agreed that he came back home a different sort of person than he'd been before. He was reclusive now, and much more somber. And he'd started hanging around with a bad crowd.

"Is your truck drivable?" Phoebe asked.

He shook his head.

"Where'd you leave it?" Phoebe asked.

"Side road."

"Is it insured?"

"I ain't worried about the truck," he snapped. Then, realizing he'd sounded sharp he mumbled, "I 'preciate yer help."

Phoebe offered to drive him home, but Leon said he'd rather walk. As he ambled off, she finished repacking her supplies, disposing of the sharps and biohazards in their respective containers. Then she got back into her Jeep and set out again.

CHAPTER 7

Ivy Iverson regained consciousness at mid-morning. She found herself splayed in a backbend with her head and feet below the level of her waist. Her head was killing her. And her back. She tried to sit up, but failed because she didn't have much strength. The effort caused the world to spin in a way that made her sick. She threw up, barely able to turn her head enough so as not to choke. Her situation was dire, even deadly. She needed to concentrate.

She could tell it was daylight, but her vision was so blurry, that was about all she could be sure of. Her body was a mix of agonizing pain and numbness. She reached around her, grasping only air. After a few panicked moments she remembered where she was and stopped thrashing.

She felt horribly sick and weak. She had no idea how long she'd been hanging there, but she knew if she didn't get her head up soon, she'd die. Somehow she had to sit up. That was her first priority.

She bent her arms and tried to fold them across her stomach. Her shoulders and hands were on fire with pins and needles, but her knuckles bumped against something that had to be the rope.

While she waited for some feeling to come back into her fingers, she tried to bring her feet together and cross her ankles, but she'd lost the ability to coordinate her leg movements. For long painful minutes, she flexed and relaxed her hands gently until she could feel the main climbing rope, then she took hold of it. Slowly, she raised herself by scooting her fists up until her shoulders were higher than her knees. This way she transferred her weight to the part of the harness that wrapped around her legs.

Once she was sitting upright, she leaned her face against the rope, feeling herself sway. Then, without any warning, she vomited again. Now she was wearing the contents of her stomach all over herself, but in the state she was in, that was the least of her problems.

It took many tries, but eventually she was able to clumsily work the zipper of her jacket and fasten it around both herself and the rope. This would hold her upright. She tried to raise her hood, but couldn't lift her arms higher than her chest. Before she could wonder about who wanted to kill her and why, she grew faint.

Her last conscious thought was that her personal paradise had gone to hell and she had no idea if she'd be able to make it out alive.

CHAPTER 8

The Smokies landscape lay like a rumpled rug some giant had tripped on. No matter where you were going, you had to climb over ridges and then dip down into hollows, over and over again. Cell phone service in the hollows was spotty to say the least. Phoebe would be out of range of a tower for awhile, but when she crested a ridge she might enter an area with service. When this occurred several calls would come in at once.

Sure enough, as Phoebe topped Walnut Ridge, her phone chirped. She put the Jeep in park so she wouldn't lose the signal while she returned a batch of calls. They were all from Waneeta.

Waneeta was the dispatcher at Southern Appalachian Home Health Care where Phoebe worked. Waneeta was a lovely person burdened with a name her mother liked the sound of, but had no idea was spelled J-u-a-n-i-t-a. Terrible spelling was pretty common in White Oak, Tennessee.

She dialed her office.

"Hey there, sister," Phoebe said.

"Where are ye?" Waneeta asked.

"Walnut Ridge."

"What're ye doin *there*?"

"I just escaped from Wanda's house. I mean that literally. We had a serious difference of opinion over her course of treatment."

Waneeta laughed.

"Then I found Leon Lowery in the road and I had to patch him up."

"They," Waneeta said, using the local dialect's gentle substitute for an expletive and drawing the word out, but then her diction and topic made a sudden U-turn.

"What color is the discharge? Does it have a foul odor? Well here's what you need to do, get a real sharp...."

Phoebe wasn't bothered by the *non sequitur*, knowing this sort of monologue meant Bruce, their boss, had come out of his office and Waneeta was employing a favorite tactic to make him go away.

Waneeta, four times married and divorced, was a world-class manipulator of men and Bruce was notoriously squeamish. It was child's play for her to send him running with explicit talk about body fluids, private parts, or surgical procedures. The only reason a man like Bruce could become a health care executive was because health care had gone corporate and was now run by accountants and computer geeks. Doctors, nurses, and patients were little more than an unruly nuisance to the management of Appalachian Health Care, Inc.

Lucky for Phoebe and the people of White Oak, Waneeta was an equally wily manipulator of the health care system. She was a genius at the art of medical coding, knowing the right number to use to identify a diagnosis and treatment so as to get a reimbursement for the patient. Insurance companies wouldn't cover an expense unless the right hoops were jumped through. The system was neither logical nor reasonable, but Waneeta was smart, ruthless, and extremely determined. Getting reimbursement for legitimate services, whether the system was set up to provide it or not, was like a sport to her.

There was a high demand for good coders in the medical system, but, like Phoebe, Waneeta preferred the challenge of trying to take care of her own humble community rather than making three times more money working for a ritzy orthopedic surgery group in a city.

Then, just as suddenly as the conversation veered off course, it veered back again, Waneeta said, "So what happened with Wanda?"

"I'll tell you later," Phoebe said. "Let's just say we'll need to wait a *long* time before scheduling any follow-up."

"That bad?" Waneeta sighed. "Well, don't worry about it, honey. I'll think of somethin."

Phoebe consulted with a doctor about each of her calls. She was fortunate to be supervised by the local family physician who'd been her own doctor when she was growing up. Doc Coleman was in his mid-eighties now and retired except for his supervision of Phoebe.

On most weekdays they managed to have a meal together at Hamilton's Trading Center. It was the only place where the rural community could congregate.

A small group of regulars ate breakfast or lunch at the tiny café and deli that occupied a corner of the store, but sooner or later most of the rest of the inhabitants of White Oak dropped by to pick up groceries or catch up on gossip.

Hamilton's was an authentic country store that had been in the same family for more than a hundred years. It still had the original wooden floor, antique tiger oak display cabinets with ornate brass fittings, and deep floor-to-ceiling shelves that lined the wall behind a long polished oak counter.

The floors were severely warped and creaked with every step you took. The outside of the place hadn't been spruced up in so long, the sign painted onto the side of the building had faded to illegibility. All sorts of things were stacked on the front porch, placed there by the current owner's grandfather during the previous fifty years. But the old man had been much loved, so the family had never been able to bring themselves to throw any of it away.

Although it was less than a mile from the park, it wasn't the sort of place tourists would stop at. That suited the people of White Oak just fine. The café regulars were a handful of mostly middle-aged or elderly farmers, Doc, Phoebe, and anyone else who happened to be passing by at mealtime.

The store owner, Jill Walker, cooked for the restaurant and deli and lived in the back. She was married, but her husband had left years ago and hadn't been seen or heard from since.

Jill wasn't a very good cook, but she could produce edible, local ethnic cuisine. She cooked more or less as a favor to the men who didn't have anybody else to cook for them. The store and the restaurant brought in a modest income, but she made most of her money by sewing elaborate and beautiful crazy-quilted coats made from sweaters she bought on sale at thrift stores and Goodwill, earning her the nickname *Goodwill Jill.*

Doc always sat at a table in the corner and if she was able to be there, Phoebe ate with him. She'd ask his advice on tough cases and they'd swap stories.

When she was young, Doc had encouraged Phoebe to go to

college and to pursue a career in health care. He'd even given her money for books and tuition when she ran short. So when Doc needed to retire on account of his health, and no doctor could be found to take his place, it was the final bit of motivation Phoebe needed. She came home to take over as much of his practice as she could.

Now they were happy to be able to catch a meal together every day or so and revel in the trials and triumphs of providing medical care in the southern Appalachian highlands.

"Hey Doc," Phoebe said, as she pulled out a chair.

"Hello there girl," Doc said. "How're you holdin up?" Doc knew Phoebe was having a hard time and he searched her face for signs of the strain she was under.

"Pretty good," she said. "Better'n Leon anyway. I ran into him on the road this mornin. He'd had some sorta wreck and got his face all beat up. Nothin too serious."

"That boy," Doc said, shaking his head.

"I know people say all sorts of things about him," said Phoebe, "but I don't know, I just like him."

"Leon's a remarkable person," Doc mused. "His grandmother was a real special lady, too."

"I remember her," Phoebe said.

Leon had been raised by his grandmother. Not because his parents weren't good people who loved him, but because he and his granny had a special bond so he'd preferred to stay with her most of the time.

She was a well-regarded herbalist. And everyone knew she had the second sight. It ran in Leon's family. In fact, it was fairly common in the insular mountain community. Outsiders might scoff at the idea of being psychic, but the people of White Oak knew better. Phoebe suspected the mists in the Smokies conveyed not only earthly sounds, but also unearthly voices.

"He never seems to gain any weight, and I worry about that," Phoebe said. "Of course he smokes like a stack. Please let me know if you think of anything else I can do for him."

"I will," Doc said. "But you've got to keep in mind that some conditions are more resistant to treatment than others. And some problems you can't treat at all. But no matter what's going on, everybody deserves good nursing care. Sometimes that's all anybody can do, but often it helps more than anything else."

Phoebe smiled. Doc had always told her that nursing was where the rubber really met the road. It was why she'd become a nurse in the first place.

"I've had quite the morning," Phoebe said, sighing. "It's only 11 o'clock and I've already had to run for my life by way of the bathroom window."

Doc laughed. "Some house calls are a lot rougher than others," he said. "That's why doctors quit making them. What'd you get into?"

"Wanda," Phoebe said, and left it at that.

Doc nodded, "Diabetics are a different breed. It's interesting. The disease isn't just about blood sugar."

Doc had accumulated all sorts of stray bits of wisdom from observing life so closely for so many years.

"Science doesn't understand much about any disease process. Not really. We like to pretend we do, but all we actually know is how to treat some symptoms. Our science doesn't give us much meaningful information about what's actually going on."

Phoebe nodded.

"What's in a person's soul matters more than anything else, and yet we don't pay much attention to that. The simplest truth is that we're all killing ourselves with our temperament. A person will tend toward being bossy, or high-strung, or depressed, or listless. And this has predictable physical consequences. If we don't learn to become aware of our moods and take steps to moderate them, we'll eventually die from our habits. This is where heart disease, cancer, diabetes, and autoimmune problems come from."

Phoebe loved it when Doc talked like this. He was a wonderful doctor with deep and wide experience.

"I've been reading up on plant essences and essential oil therapy," he said. "It's fascinating stuff. The idea is that we can use plants as templates to nudge the soul in the right direction. Either that or we can keep behaving the same way we always have and rely on mainstream medicine to try to cope with the symptoms.

"It's pitiful really. The practice of medicine should focus more on the problems in people's hearts and minds, before the problems work their way into the body. But I don't suppose the drug companies would like that." He winked at her and added, "And we don't dare cross em, do we?"

They sat in companionable silence and pondered the medical mafia. Phoebe's glance was drawn to the window over Doc's shoulder. She noticed a flash coming from a high ridge in Greenbrier. That was odd. It was a particularly remote, nearly inaccessible area.

Jill came to the table to refresh their drinks and Phoebe pointed and said, "Wonder who's up there?"

"Nobody in their right mind," said Jill, smiling. Then she turned and looked again, serious now, and saw the flashing, too. "Lord help anybody tryin to hike way up there."

"I will lift up mine eyes unto the hills, from whence cometh my help," Doc quoted, *"My help cometh from the Lord, which made heaven and earth."*

Both Phoebe and Jill said, "Amen." Then Phoebe stood and said, "Well, I've gotta be goin."

"You take care of yourself," Doc said.

She went to the counter to pay for her meal, and Jill followed her to the register. She rang up Phoebe's lunch on an antique oak cash register, pressing down hard on the tall brass keys. The two women were friends from childhood. They'd kept in touch sporadically during the years Phoebe had been gone and now that she was back, their friendship picked up again as if she'd never left.

"You hangin in there?" Jill asked.

"Yeah," said Phoebe.

Jill looked at her with sympathy, but didn't press. "Well, call me or come by if you need anything."

Phoebe nodded.

The bell on the front door tinkled as it opened and two men walked in. It was Lester and Fate, a two-man crime wave and the bosses of White Oak's underworld. As they passed the cash register, Fate set a heavy brown paper grocery bag on the counter without saying anything, then joined his associate at their regular table beside the large front window. Jill looked in the bag. It was full of fresh tomatoes and carrots from somebody's garden. No telling whose.

Leon had been hanging around with them recently, but he wasn't with them now. "Y'all be good," Phoebe said in the general direction of the men and they nodded politely, without promising anything. Then she went out to her Jeep.

When she got in she noticed a white plastic trash bag in the passenger seat that hadn't been there before. She peeked inside. It was full of exotic new antibiotics that were a week or so past their expiration date. It was thousands of dollars worth of pills and capsules.

God bless those hoods, she thought, whichever of them it was who stole the medicine for her. She hoped they hadn't hurt anybody to get it. Oh well, she didn't have time right now to worry with imaginary problems, she had real ones to think about. She'd put it off as long as possible, but now she'd have to face one of them head-on.

She had to go to Sean's funeral.

CHAPTER 9

Phoebe had been dating for a very long time without ever losing faith that there was someone out there somewhere who was perfect for her. And she figured they were searching for her. But even the most optimistic people had their limits. Today she was seriously considering giving up on men altogether.

Neither she nor her most recent ex-boyfriend could be blamed for this current romantic disaster. She pondered whether at age fifty-four the entire concept of dating wasn't downright unseemly. She asked herself this as she stood next to the grave of the man she'd been on a date with last Saturday, a mere four days ago. He was her latest, now *late* in the worst possible way, boyfriend Sean.

She couldn't really take it in yet, still couldn't feel much beyond numb shock, but she knew she'd miss Sean. He'd been a *character*, to use the local euphemism that covered a mind-boggling array of quirks, but he was kind and thoughtful and Phoebe had learned to value these qualities over looks and income-producing capacity.

In keeping with Sean's distinctive personal style, his burial was taking place atop a high bald knob in the Great Smoky Mountains National Park amid half a million acres of wilderness. Getting there was no problem for Sean, but it made things tough on his mourners because the highest elevations of the Smokies were cloud forests and fog forests, places as damp as rainforests but at an altitude where the water tended to remain airborne. Today the endlessly playful sky was in exuberant form, bombarding Sean's friends and family with alternating mist, fog, clouds, and light rain.

Phoebe's mind was mirroring the weather, leaping uncontrollably from one topic to another. She struggled to follow the prayers that were being read, but for some reason a bizarre idea kept recurring no matter how forcefully she repressed it. It was the notion that this would make a fantastic pilot episode for a television series called *Xtreme Funerals*. Phoebe didn't even own a television, but she knew lots of people watched shows like that.

It had everything. It was taking place in an exclusive setting in one of the world's top vacation spots. The service was being spoken in the singsong cadences of the local dialect, a patois of old speech brought from England, Scotland, and Ireland, in an accent that would be largely unintelligible to outsiders.

She looked at her fellow mourners. Not one person was wearing traditional funeral garb. It wasn't disrespect for Sean, it was just practical considering the logistics. Instead of black there were a lot of bright splashes of color from the high-tech hiking gear necessary to stay relatively comfortable while traveling on foot three miles horizontally and a thousand feet vertically from the parking lot through an Appalachian jungle and back again.

If you were out for several hours in the higher elevations of the Smokies, it was inevitable that you'd get rained on. And if you weren't dressed for that in layers topped off with breathable waterproofing, you were likely to get hypothermia, even in the middle of summer.

Sean's funeral attendance looked like Outward Bound meets Protestant descendants of Druids, but there was also a Mexican family he'd befriended.

She couldn't believe shameful thoughts like this were filling her head. They'd only been going out for a month and a half, but still, she owed him more internal decorum than he was getting. She wondered how many others in the sober-faced crowd were also lost in a tangle of idiotic thoughts.

Fog swirled around Phoebe's feet, obscuring the ground. Hours earlier, dawn had lent an encouraging pink glow to the mist-enshrouded landscape, in God's version of those special light bulbs you could buy to make your complexion look better. But now that the sun was higher it was turning the fog to a dirty white that blurred the edges of everything.

Thirty-eight years ago when she'd gone on her first date Phoebe never imagined that she'd work her way through a succession of boyfriends that progressed from sweet sixteen until one of them would actually die.

Did any young girl picture herself moving from slender teen guys who didn't need to shave, to men whose dinner conversation revolved around prostate and bladder problems? She doubted it.

She dared not try to imagine her future. Not right now anyway. The preacher read from the King James Bible. The cadences of it pervaded life in White Oak.

"Lord, thou hast been our dwelling place in all generations. Before the mountains were brought forth, or ever thou hadst formed the earth and the world, even from everlasting to everlasting, thou art God."

The fog whirled away leaving a gap just in time for everyone to see Sean's ashes being deposited with somber ceremony into a narrow hole dug between where his parents lay in one of the oldest graveyards in the national park. His mother had come from one of the thousand families who'd been ejected from their farms in the 30's when the park was created.

A few descendants of these original families still had the right to be buried in the family plots. But in these areas where all signs of habitation had been removed and wilderness allowed to reclaim the land, no more gravestones or even modifications to gravestones were allowed. There would never be any indication of Sean's presence here. Not even a Post-It note on his parents' headstone. That seemed harsh, but Phoebe didn't think Sean would mind. He'd been a very low-key guy.

"Like as a father pitieth his children, so the Lord pitieth them that fear him. For he knoweth our frame; he remembereth that we are dust. As for man, his days are as grass: as a flower of the field, so he flourisheth. For the wind passeth over it, and it is gone; and the place thereof shall know it no more. But the mercy of the Lord is from everlasting to everlasting...."

Sean had been an only child. His closest next-of-kin were double first cousins and they were good people. They made it easy on the pallbearers by having Sean cremated and then they thoughtfully dug the hole for his ashes ahead of time with a posthole digger from Sean's own barn. Sean would've appreciated that touch. Like all men everywhere, he loved his tools. But even with all the manual labor taken care of, it was still an ordeal for everyone to hike the steep, muddy, and rocky trail to get to the graveyard. And it would be a sweaty, messy trip back.

Phoebe wondered if Sean's death confirmed her as a spinster, an old maid. She wasn't bothered by the old maid label because she knew women like her might be old, but most of them were less of a maid in any sense of the word than other women. Phoebe had been through a long string of men and hadn't cleaned up after any of them. She'd dated all kinds.

Phoebe knew deep down that the real reason she'd never gotten married was that she'd never met a man she believed was capable of honoring marriage vows. Maybe nobody could. But Phoebe had been hurt the same way over and over again until she'd lost her optimism about the notion of a permanent commitment.

She didn't want to be bitter about it. She tried to accept that men were just different from women and leave it at that. She knew she was lucky in that she enjoyed her own company and made enough money to get by on, so she hadn't been forced to shackle herself for social or financial reasons to someone she couldn't trust.

Sean had never been married either. She stared at the small circular seam in the sod that carpeted his tiny new bachelor pad. Then she swiveled her head to take in the surroundings. It was early October and the leaves were still on the nearby trees. Just a hint of red touched the sumac and blackberry.

In a couple of weeks though, the place would be afire with yellow, orange, purple, and red. Tourists would flock to the area to enjoy the world famous spectacle as the color started at the top of the mountains and then gradually slid downhill for a month or so until the show was over and the leaves were all on the ground.

"For I am persuaded, that neither death, nor life, nor angels, nor principalities, nor powers, nor things present, nor things to come, Nor height, nor depth, nor any other creature, shall be able to separate us from the love of God, which is in Christ Jesus our Lord."

Exotic vapors swirled through the crowd again, making sounds bounce and echo eerily. Suddenly Phoebe found herself standing in a mini-whiteout. She and the grave were enveloped in a cloud. She'd been standing alongside a dozen others, then they'd all vanished. While the cloud wafted past, she seemed to be alone.

Maybe it was a metaphor for her life from this point on. She was all alone in the world. The notion made her cry. She took a deep breath of the nearly liquid air and felt cool droplets of moisture condense onto her hot face. It was a comforting counterpoint to her tears. She wondered if this cloud-out might be what heaven was like. Maybe angels didn't bother to dry anybody's tears, but simply drowned them out with something useful, like rain. Something that could do the world some good.

While wrapped in her own personal cloud, Phoebe tried to concentrate on the bright side. The most obvious plus in this situation was that mercifully for Sean, he hadn't suffered. He'd been out walking, fallen, hit his head on a rock, and died instantly.

Phoebe knew most people weren't that lucky. Most people suffered.

It was strange that he'd been out in the woods, because she'd never known him to go hiking, but there were no signs of foul play. And he wasn't the kind of guy who had enemies. She tried not to be paranoid.

Over the years she'd had countless patients pass away and even some friends, too, but she'd never lost a boyfriend to death. Just when she thought she'd seen it all, she had a brand new reason to cry over a breakup.

"And God shall wipe away all tears from their eyes; and there shall be no more death, neither sorrow, nor crying, neither shall there be any more pain: for the former things are passed away."

She'd learned a long time ago that she couldn't trust men much, but she used to at least be able to depend on them to stay alive until they got tired of her and cheated, and she caught them and broke up. And yet, four days ago one of them had gone from being *hot* to being *not* in the blink of an eye.

She knew it wasn't fair to blame Sean for dying, but it was annoying to keep having to adjust her standards down. Honestly, what was left when you couldn't count on a man to maintain vital signs? Was she still asking too much?

"Peace I leave with you, my peace I give unto you: not as the world giveth, give I unto you. Let not your heart be troubled, neither let it be afraid."

Phoebe would try to keep that last bit of advice in mind.

CHAPTER 10

After the service was over the mourners headed back down the trail. Phoebe was the last to leave, or at least she'd thought she was. She finished saying goodbye to Sean and prepared to make a long solitary walk back to her car. But when she turned to leave, she saw the group's official escort from the National Park Service was still there. She read the nametag on his ranger uniform: *H. Matthews*. Then she looked at his face. Good grief, it was Henry.

She was shocked and embarrassed that she hadn't noticed him earlier. They'd gone to school together and even been sweethearts when they were children, but she hadn't seen him in years. In fact, she wasn't sure she would've known who he was unless she'd seen his badge. He must've had to wait for her so he could be sure everybody got back safely.

Without saying anything, Henry started down the trail. Maybe he didn't recognize her. Phoebe raised the hood on her jacket and followed him. It was going to be a wet trip back. The mist was giving way to rain again. The vegetation dripped onto them from overhead and shed water every time they brushed against it.

Neither of them spoke for a long time. They'd both spent a large part of their lives playing in woods like these, so they were comfortable with the sound of the rain and the smells of the forest.

Their boots thudded and vibrated against the ground as they clomped down the steep trail. The footing was precarious on account of slippery mud, jagged rocks, and gnarled roots exposed by the lugs on thousands of pairs of heavy hiking boots and decades of rushing water.

"I'm real sorry about your friend dyin," said Henry, as he held a branch out of the way.

"Thank you," Phoebe said. "So am I. He was a nice fella."

They walked some more, then Phoebe said, "Do you have to go to a lot of burials?"

"Not too many," he replied.

"Sean's cousins gave him a nice send-off, didn't they?"

"Yeah," he said, "they sure did."

As they descended from the high to the mid-elevations, the cold rain stopped, the sun came out, and curling tendrils of nearly transparent smoke rose from the ground as the water evaporated.

"His cousins said it took more paperwork to get him buried in the park than on the White House lawn," Phoebe said.

Henry nodded his agreement.

"I guess whenever the government's involved," Phoebe said, "there's always a lot of paperwork."

"That's true," Henry said. "There are all kinda rules and regulations for buryin somebody in the park."

They came to a blowdown where a huge tree lay across the trail. Henry climbed over it and Phoebe stooped to go underneath. Henry reached under the trunk and took her hand to steady her so she wouldn't have to crawl and get her knees muddy.

"There's a reason for restrictions on burials in the park," he said.

"What is it?"

He let go of her hand, but stood looking at her with concern, and said, "You don't really wanna talk about this kinda thing right now, do ye?"

"Sure I do," she said. "We've got another forty-five minutes of walkin ahead of us."

Henry smiled. The mischievous sense of humor so prevalent in the community was blazing from his eyes and suddenly all the years and all the sadness dropped away from Phoebe and they were just kids again, playing in the woods.

"There's millions of people roamin around in this park," he said as he turned away from her and resumed walking. "You wouldn't *believe* what kinda stuff they get up to."

"Like what?"

"Like throwin out a bag of ashes on the upwind side of a full picnic ground and gettin little flakes of granny all over people's tater salad."

Phoebe snorted. "Good Lord, can't they even step into the woods?" Ten feet into the verdant Smokies would put them totally out of view behind a screen of vegetation.

"No," he said, shaking his head. "Eighty-five percent of the visitors to the park never get more than fifty yards from their car. There's about 900 miles of trails and 2,100 miles of rivers and creeks, but nearly everbody's trompin around on the same little bald patches of dirt."

They both laughed.

"I can't see the reasonin behind bringin yer loved one's ashes to the park just so you can toss em out onto the asphalt," he said. "But that's what people do, time after time. And that's just *one* example. We've caught em puttin ashes in a creek a few feet upstream from swimmin holes where little kids are splashin around or right above where some fool's fillin up a canteen!"

Phoebe laughed so hard that it made her lose her footing. She had to windmill her arms to stay upright. "I thought people knew better than to drink outta these creeks nowadays."

"Well they don't. They come here from God knows where so they can indulge a fantasy about drinkin fresh cold mountain spring water, but they're actually drinkin the used toilet and bath water from wild hogs."

Phoebe was laughing and smiling now and Henry was glad he was able to take her mind off her sadness. If tourist escapades made her feel better, he was happy to oblige. Thirty years spent wrangling people and critters had given him an endless supply of material.

"Lord, Phoebe, sometimes they don't even take the ashes outta the container! We've found sealed plastic bags full of ashes layin right in the middle of a creek, stickin up in plain view of a scenic overlook. But when they do *that*, we can catch em. People don't realize there's a little metal tag inside the packages that identifies the deceased.

"When we get hold of that tag, we can track down the survivin family and find out who did it. I can't understand it, but even with the ones who manage to get the container open, sometimes we find the little metal tags layin right in or beside the trail, or the fisheries people see em flashin in the creek. We go after those people, too."

"That's pitiful," Phoebe said.

"Well, I guess if they're lucky, people don't have much experience disposin of human remains," Henry said. "You'd hope only a professional would get practice at it. And the amateurs are doin it when they're the most upset they've ever been in their lives. So I guess there's a lot of potential for mistakes.

"And the survivor's likely to be old and female. That plastic is real strong and an elderly woman's too weak to tear it open bare handed. And too frail to wade into a creek to fish the old man out and try again."

Phoebe laughed and said, "That's true."

"It gets worse," Henry said. "Sometimes a ridge runner'll find a brand new headstone right alongside the Appalachian Trail! If we didn't police it, Phoebe, there'd be dead people layin all over the most popular places in the park. We'd have eight hundred square miles of wilderness ringed with mass graves!"

Phoebe snorted with laughter.

"Then there's the memorial tree people," he said. "You wouldn't believe how many requests we get ever year to plant a memorial tree in one of the few little bits of lawn we've got in the public areas. The biggest hardwood forest on the face of the earth ain't enough. They wanna plant one more tree, usually an invasive species, with a commemorative plaque, and they want it right in front of a Visitor Center."

"Why not plant the tree in a place where people'd need em?" Phoebe asked.

"I don't know! I'm sure they mean well. It's just that people *love* this park beyond reason. And they want to do somethin nice for the dead person, but they just don't think it through."

Phoebe reflected on how hard it was to be dignified, especially for hillbillies, and even more for a group of hillbillies. A cluster of hillbillies was a volatile mix. They were combustible in so many ways, both comic and violent, often both at the same time. They were an unpredictably impulsive lot. She knew because she was a purebred one herself, eleventh generation born in the USA.

To be a full-blooded hillbilly was to be a living *koan*. Half of you wanted to be dignified and half of you couldn't tolerate any restraint. You could see it in the regional art and hear it in the music. Wood carving with chainsaws. Cloggers who danced up a storm with the lower half of their bodies, but held the upper half perfectly still and stared off into the distance stone-faced. Or a group of bluegrass musicians who'd be playing the most raucous tunes imaginable, looking around at each other with bemused expressions that seemed to say *where's all that racket comin from?*

Phoebe believed that nearly all the adult males everywhere were pretty much the same way. Most of them could manage to keep the top half of themselves under a semblance of control, but the bottom half tended to run wild. As she continued to descend the trail she couldn't help but think that most men were mentally ill below the waist.

CHAPTER 11

It was turning out to be a pretty day by the time Phoebe and Henry made it back to the parking lot. They stood next to Phoebe's car chatting until Henry sensed she was stalling.

"I've gotta go over to Cataloochee to check on a bear trap," he said, "and I need to change out the batteries on an elk's collar if I can find him. You're welcome to ride along."

"I wouldn't wanna to be in the way," Phoebe said.

"You won't. I could use an extra pair of hands. But it's a long drive across the mountain and we won't get back here til late."

Phoebe looked at her feet. She had the rest of the day off. She thought about going home and sitting alone with her cat, and trying not to cry over Sean. "That'd be great."

Henry was driving his work vehicle, a white Ford Explorer he'd parked military style, facing out. The doors bore the dark green seal of the Department of the Interior. Phoebe wondered why it was called that. Shouldn't it be the Department of the Exterior?

The truck was outfitted with a radio like the ones the police used. Henry kept it tuned to a channel that was like a party line where they could listen in on the chitchat of rangers from all over the park with a central dispatcher. Phoebe had trouble following what they were talking about, though, because they used code.

When a disembodied male voice reported a 507 and asked for instructions, Phoebe asked, "What's a 507?"

"A bear jam," Henry said.

The phrase meant nothing to her. She pondered the unfamiliar term. Was it a music festival in the park, or were bears actually playing instruments like the birds at Parrot Jungle? Maybe it was when a bunch of bears tried to cram into a small space. Somewhere she'd heard that a gang of bears was called a sloth or a sleuth, but she wondered who in their right minds would ever talk like that.

Her post-funeral train of thought seemed destined to continue on an idiotic downward spiral, so she asked, "What's a bear jam?"

"Oh, it's a traffic jam caused by tourists who're lookin at a bear. People get excited when they see one so they'll stop to take a look. Lots of times they don't even pull over. They just put the car in park and leave it sittin in the middle of the road while they walk around to get a better view or take pictures. If one car stops on a one-lane road, everybody behind it has to stop too. The traffic gets backed up for miles.

"And of course some people aren't satisfied with lookin from a distance. They try to get up close or bait the bear with food, or, if they're drunk, they might try to chase one."

"People *chase* bears?" Phoebe was incredulous.

"If they're drunk enough."

The national park had only a few interior roads so it was common to have to take a long convoluted route to get somewhere that wasn't very far away as the crow flies. To get to the Cataloochee

Valley, which was across the mountains in North Carolina, Henry explained that they had to take secondary roads to I-40, go to North Carolina, then turn back toward Tennessee and drive along a notoriously curvy one-lane gravel road.

They'd driven for about fifteen minutes when the radio sputtered a message for Henry. "Dispatch to Matthews, what's your 20?"

"Matthews to Dispatch, I'm traveling east on Little River Road."

"Dispatch to Matthews, divert to Cades Cove and rendezvous with Sanders at the Cantilever Barn."

"Matthews to Dispatch, roger that."

Henry stopped, executed a perfect three-point turn, and headed back the way they'd come.

"Sanders is a seasonal ranger," Henry explained.

"What's goin on?"

"I don't know, but when they don't give any details, its bad news. Something they don't wanna say over the airwaves. People monitor our radios with scanners. So if there's somethin dispatch doesn't want tourists or the press to hear, they don't say it. Looks like Cataloochee will have to wait for now."

CHAPTER 12

The backpack had been dropped off where it was certain to be found and the crossbow and other gear had been stashed in the opposite sort of place. Now he needed to move Ivy's car. In order to do that he had to walk down Greenbrier Road, find her car, and get in it. There was no way to do this without getting out in the open for anyone and everyone to see.

He was tired and his legs were killing him from the miles of steep hiking he'd done that day. And he was sore from his wounds. But he was cleaned up now so you'd hardly notice the cuts. As cars drove by, he gave them a friendly smile and nod. Most of the traffic was from hikers leaving either Porters Creek Trail or Ramsey Cascades. A few people had used the pull-offs so they could stroll along the Middle Prong of Little Pigeon River.

He had Ivy's keys so all he had to do was walk a few hundred yards, then move the car to a nearby campground parking lot. Left overnight at a trailhead it wouldn't take long for it to stand out. But in a campground parking lot it would take days before it was noticed.

He spotted the Toyota Land Cruiser easily. With its roof-mounted luggage rack, it was easily the tallest vehicle in the lot.

He looked up and squinted at the cloudless blue sky. It was

turning out to be a beautiful day.

It was early afternoon when Henry and Phoebe reached Cades Cove. The cove was a beloved and heavily-touristed area where the lifestyle of the people who'd been ejected to build the park was preserved as an outdoor museum. There was a picturesque hodgepodge of historic log cabins, barns, and prim white churches. It was a rustic, Disney-esque Appalachia with no electricity or cell phone service.

The cove was the most popular area of the most popular national park in the country. Two million people a year drove the one-lane, one-way, 11-mile loop road. It was an idyllic-looking place that covered 6,800 acres. Nearly a third of it was priceless flat, cleared land surrounded and protected by a ring of misty blue mountain ridges.

"There's about 1,500 bears in the park," Henry said, "but they're not spread out evenly. Unfortunately they're drawn to the areas where people are because they smell food."

Phoebe nodded, she knew tourists feeding bears was a huge problem.

"Bears only have a few months a year to gain all the weight they're gonna need to stay alive during the winter and early spring. We're far enough south that they don't go into full hibernation here, but they do have a semi-hibernation from about November to March or April. The males go in last and come out first. The females stay in longer cause they're givin birth and nursin cubs in the dens.

"When the bears first wake up and come out of their dens in

the early spring, there's not much to eat. They have to find a way to survive somehow for a few months until the berries get ripe. Then a few months later, if it's been a good year for acorns, that's when they have plenty to eat and can get nice and fat."

"Is that what they're doin now?" Phoebe asked.

"Yeah. In the fall, just before they go into their dens, they get desperate. They eat all day long every day, tryin to store up as much fat as they can. In a year where the acorn crop fails, it's terrible for the bears. That's the sort of thing that makes em overcome their natural fear of humans and come into the populated areas to try to find food.

"If that happens, we have problems. The bears in this park aren't real mean, but people are unpredictable when they see one, so it's a lot safer for the bears if we can keep them away from the populated areas."

They topped a rise as they entered the cove and the splendid panorama made famous by millions of postcards, refrigerator magnets, and tourist photos was spread out before them.

"Holy moly, look at that traffic," said Phoebe.

"Yep," said Henry, "that's a bear jam."

Vehicles of all sorts were bumper-to-bumper as far as the eye could see. Traffic was at a complete standstill. People had their car doors thrown open and children were running to and fro.

Henry pointed to a rusty gate set in the edge of the woods next to the road, handed Phoebe a small key, and asked her to open it for him. "And lock it back after I go through."

She did as he asked, then got back in the truck, and tried to give him back the key. "Keep it," he said, "you'll need it again in a few minutes."

They drove along a dirt track through the woods, then came out into the bright, sunny open fields. Phoebe could see a barn in the distance and also a log cabin nearby with a huge crowd. "That's the Carter-Shields cabin," said Henry. "That's prob'ly where the problem is, but we'll start out at a less crowded spot."

They came to another gate, which Phoebe opened and closed. Now they were back to the paved loop road, which was hopelessly blocked by dozens of cars whose drivers and passengers had abandoned them. Henry crept down the narrow shoulder of the road and parked the SUV.

The crowd was in distinct clusters. The largest group was milling around the cabin and the surrounding lawn. Some of them were watching volunteers demonstrating old-time crafts like a mule-drawn sorghum molasses press and broom-making.

Another cluster of tourists, these with cameras, were congregating near a mother and two cubs. The experienced photographers stood well back from the animals at a safe distance with long-lensed cameras mounted on tripods.

There were dozens of people doing an extremely poor job of trying to sneak up on the wild animals while wearing gaudy colored clothing and stage-whispering to each other. They were standing in a slight crouch an inch or two less than their normal height. It was a ludicrous sight.

The family of bears was browsing for food. Phoebe was no expert, but some of the tourists seemed to be getting *way* too close to the bears. Several of them had small children with them. What were they thinking? Didn't they understand the concept of a wild animal? A big wild animal with huge teeth and claws, and the capacity to kill them if it felt threatened? Obviously not.

One of the professional photographers was waving at Henry and Henry headed toward him. Phoebe trailed along behind. When Henry got close, the man stepped back and indicated that he should take a look through the camera and its telescopic lens. Henry stooped and peered through the viewfinder. "A backpack?" Henry asked, surprised.

"Yeah," said the photographer.

Henry turned around and said, "Bill, this is my friend Phoebe. Phoebe this is Bill Lawson. He's a famous bear photographer."

Bill and Phoebe shook hands.

"Did you see how she got it?" he asked.

"She just happened on it a couple of minutes ago. It was lying out there in the field. I don't know how it got there, but, Henry, there's a brown stain on it that looks like it might be dried blood."

Henry stooped and took another long look at the mother bear mauling the bright purple fabric.

"Thanks, Bill. I appreciate your help," Henry said. "Phoebe, I need you to stay here. I gotta do some work.

"I'm gonna have to get the momma to send her cubs up a tree and then dart her so I can get that pack," Henry said. "I'll have to take all three of em back to the wildlife building til we figure out what's happened. I'm real sorry, Phoebe. I'll be tied up for the rest of the day. But I'll find somebody to take you back to your car."

"Don't worry, Henry," Bill said. "I'll be happy to take her wherever she needs to go."

"Thanks," Henry said. "And Phoebe, I apologize."

"It's no problem," Phoebe said.

Henry turned and walked quickly toward his truck.

"You don't mind if we stay awhile longer, do you?" asked Bill. "I hate to leave Henry alone with em," he said, pointing at the throng of tourists. "This is gonna get ugly."

CHAPTER 13

Henry walked toward the bears and the cluster of tourists who were surrounding them. "Back away from the bears, please," he said in a calm authoritative voice.

There was some grumbling, but when they got a look at Henry's uniform and flat-brimmed Stetson hat, they put a lid on it. Phoebe suspected the minute he looked away they'd go right back.

"Do any of you know whose backpack that is that the bear is foolin with?" Henry said in a voice loud enough to be heard by everyone.

There were some head shakes, but nobody spoke up.

"Did anybody see who dropped it or gave it to the bear?"

Again, more head shaking and some murmurs, but nobody answered.

"Is anybody hurt or missin that you know of?"

At that, the buzz in the crowd got louder, but nobody offered any answers.

"You're breakin the law by intentionally approaching the bears," Henry said. "Back up right now, all the way to the road, or I'll see that every one of you gets a ticket.

"It's illegal in this park to intentionally approach a bear or any wild animal within fifty yards or any distance that disturbs the animal. I don't want to see any of you ever get this close to a bear again."

The group backed up until it merged with a growing crowd of spectators emerging from their cars, trying to see what was going on. There were at least 200 people watching when Henry went to his SUV and opened the back. Fortunately, he had his animal immobilization kit and gun, because he'd planned to use it for darting the elk to change its collar. Out of the view of the crowd, he loaded up two tranquilizer darts, took the special rifle out of it case, and loaded it.

He keyed his walkie-talkie, told dispatch as much as he cared to say over an open line, and asked for backup ASAP. Things were going to get dicey and he knew the focus was going to be on him, but there was nothing he could do about it. He couldn't wait for reinforcements, either. He had to get the backpack before it was damaged any further and he had to capture the bear family before they left the area. Once they disappeared into the woods, he might never be able to find them again.

The mother bear and cubs would have to be detained until Henry knew if they'd been involved in hurting or killing someone. If they had, he'd have to euthanize the whole family. Bears were smart. They learned from each other, even if they saw a behavior just one time, they'd remember it. He couldn't leave a bear loose in the park that was unafraid to make physical contact with a person, particularly aggressive or deadly physical contact.

He came out from behind the truck with the rifle and a collective gasp went up from the crowd. At first people moved back even farther, but he knew that wouldn't last long. He walked quickly toward the mother bear making loud huffing noises and shooing gestures. The big black bear saw that Henry was serious and grunted, signaling her cubs to climb up a nearby tree and stay there til she called them to come back down. The cubs obeyed her instantly and scampered up the side of the large tree so quickly the crowd *oh'd* and *ah'd*.

Henry quickly took aim and fired at the mother bear. The crack of the dart gun, like that of a .22 caliber rifle, cut through the cove. The bear looked surprised and then reared up on her hind legs and growled, brandishing her formidable claws and snapping her jaws. She remained like that for a few moments, then wobbled, and fell forward into a heap.

The tourists were horrified. As far as they knew, Henry had just killed Yogi in front of two little Boo Boos as their own kids looked on. They were not happy campers.

Henry headed back toward his vehicle with the intention of bringing it close to the mother bear. But he was intercepted by the crowd.

"You didn't have to kill her," a woman shouted. "She wasn't hurting anything!" Little children were wailing as their parents dragged them back toward their cars.

"I didn't kill the bear," Henry said, "I just immobilized her so I could recover the backpack she was chewin on."

"What about those two precious little babies you just orphaned!" a woman called. "You gonna leave them to starve now?"

The heckling and catcalls quickly turned to mild jostling as Henry tried to make his way through the crowd.

Many of the spectators were using cell phones or iPads to take photos and video. Others were attempting to text, tweet, or phone their friends.

It took only a couple of minutes for the mob to realize they weren't able to get a cell phone connection. Some of the people, furious at being thwarted by the lack of cell phone service, started pushing and shoving.

"Hey, one more push out of anyone and your vacation is going to end up in an arrest!" Henry barked, shielding the remaining dart with his body. The medicine in the dart would sedate a bear, but it would kill a human.

Although there was no cell phone service, the rangers' radios worked inside the cove, unless the repeater happened to be down for maintenance. Lucky for Henry, the radio tower was working fine today.

He made a beeline for his SUV and with his threat of arrest still hanging in the air the crowds grudgingly parted before him. Bill and Phoebe met him in front of the truck.

"I've gotta call a wildlife tech and law enforcement rangers over here," Henry said to both of them as he grabbed for the radio in the truck.

"You're bleeding!" Phoebe said incredulously.

"That happens sometimes," Henry said

"You get attacked by *tourists*?"

"Ill-behaved tourists are the alpha predators in this park. They're way more aggressive than any of the animals. Animals will generally leave you alone."

"Have you got a first aid kit?" Phoebe asked.

Henry nodded and pointed as he made contact on the radio and requested help.

"Sit down for a moment please," Phoebe said, gently guiding him to sit on the edge of the cargo area. It was the second time today she'd made the same gesture. First Leon and now Henry. It was bizarre; she was spending the day burying one friend and triaging two others.

"I need to go get that bear quick, before she wakes up," protested Henry.

"I'm surprised you got out of that alive," Bill said, only half-joking. "I wouldn't go back over there until the others get here."

"I can't believe some of those people," Phoebe said, as she dabbed at cuts and scratches on Henry's forearms. "That was uncalled for."

He looked at her and grimaced. "I'm embarrassed you saw that."

"Henry, this mornin I had to leave a house call through the bathroom window. I was runnin from a woman who wanted her doughnuts back. And I thought I had it rough."

He winced as she cleaned a scratch on his face with peroxide.

Two more National Park Service vehicles pulled up, followed by a couple of volunteers in a low emission vehicle sporting a huge pair of elk antlers mounted over the windshield. Henry quickly made his way over to them with Phoebe and Bill in tow and briefed everyone on the situation.

"We need to take the bears to the wildlife building and hold em til we can figure out what's happened," he said. "If nobody's been hurt, we can bring em back and release em to go about their business.

"But first, we need to get that crowd dispersed, and second, we need to get that backpack."

Dispersing the crowd and tranquilizing the cubs with a dart pistol didn't take long. When Henry was able to examine the remnants of the mangled backpack he agreed with Bill that it had what appeared to be dried blood on it, which was not a good sign.

"I'm so sorry to have gotten you into this," Henry said, looking back at Phoebe. "I hope you'll give me another chance on that trip to Cataloochee."

"It's no problem," said Phoebe, "I've seen more than enough for one day."

"Where's your car?" Bill asked her.

"At the parking lot for the old McBride graveyard," Phoebe said. "Do you know how to get there? I'm so turned around I have no idea where it is from here."

"Oh, sure."

"Thanks Bill," Henry said, "and Phoebe, I'll be seein you later."

"Okay Henry. Be careful."

Bill and Phoebe began picking their way across the trampled trash-filled grass. "What a mess," Bill said. He leaned down to pick up a partially-eaten biscuit and put it in the bear proof dumpster. "The people who did this were upset about how the bears were being treated, but now the Park Service is gonna have to send rangers to clean up all this right away or more bears'll be comin down here to eat the garbage they left."

"I've seen people like this before," Phoebe said. "I used to work in Washington."

"You did?" Bill said, looking at her with surprise. "You sound local."

"I *am* local," Phoebe said, smiling. "I left here after college, chasin a dream I got from watchin too much television. Took me a long time, but one day I woke up and realized I wanted to come back home. Anyway, you meet a lot of activists in Washington. They're usually angry people. When you fix one issue, they immediately switch to another. It's endless. No satisfaction can ever be had. They're chronically enraged and looking for a place to vent it."

"Psychologists call that *projection* I believe," said Bill. "How do you know Henry?"

"We grew up together," Phoebe said. "Hadn't seen each other in thirty years til we ran into each other a coupla hours ago. When we figured out who each other was, he was kind enough to offer to let me ride around with him for the rest of the day."

"He's a good man," said Bill. "Those people have no idea that the man they're throwing things at is the very last person in the world they should be mad at. Ignorance is not pretty. The guy's a legend around here.

"He's a martyr to the wildlife in the Smokies. The Park Service forces rangers to rotate to different parks so they don't get attached to any particular place, but Henry refused to do it.

"He loves it here too much to leave. Unfortunately the NPS is run like a military organization and Henry's too strong-minded to follow rules that don't make sense. So he doesn't get along very well with the Park Superintendent. His refusal to knuckle under means he's always on the verge of getting court-martialed. So he's been kept in a subsistence-level job for most of his career.

"There's not much money allocated to wildlife management, but everybody knows Henry so they'll call him and he'll go out all hours of the day and night if an animal's in trouble or causing problems anywhere in the park. He'll go find it and take it to the vet hospital or move it to a safer area. He's been living like that for most of his life. Not many women would put up with that, which is probably why he's never gotten married. He's married to his job."

CHAPTER 14

Ivy's attacker moved her car, then he backtracked a few miles and recovered his own vehicle. Next on his *to-do* list was searching her apartment. He mused about what an unexpectedly action-packed and exhausting day it was turning out to be.

Ivy lived in a low-rise building in Sequoyah Hills. The place was popular with students, and there were sufficient comings and goings to render one person more or less unremarkable, he hoped. He carried a crowbar tucked up into the sleeve of his jacket, and a pair of gloves in his pockets.

He got in quickly without being seen, but the manner of his entry meant the latch wouldn't work anymore. Once he was inside he had to prop a book against the door to hold it closed while he searched the place.

Ivy wasn't much of a housekeeper, but even in the messy state she'd left the apartment, it was obvious after a few minutes that what he was looking for wasn't there.

That was unwelcome news, but not totally unanticipated. Fortunately there was another place to look.

It was mid-afternoon when Bill dropped Phoebe off at her car, but she still wasn't ready to go home, so she went back to Hamilton's to sit with her friend Jill. She knew at this time of day Jill would be sewing.

Jill made wearable art for women in a spare room she'd converted into a studio. Over the past few years, she'd built up a clientele on Etsy.com and now sewing was her primary source of income. Her sweater coats were highly sought-after, particularly by middle-aged women. The reconstructed clothes were metaphors for their lives. Jill took clothes other people had thrown away, cut out the worn and damaged places, salvaged the best parts, and reconfigured the leftovers into something practical and pretty.

Her designs were a modern retooling of an Appalachian icon, like Joseph's coat of many colors or Dolly Parton's homemade coat made famous in a country song. What had been an embarrassing necessity for the very poor, making recycled clothes out of scraps, was now the province of fiber art collectors and had been renamed *upcycling* or *eco-couture*.

Jill's intention was that her creations be unique and cheerful talismans for women going through menopause, divorce, illness, or any other life situation when resurrection by bootstraps was required.

Phoebe knocked on the doorjamb and said, "Can I come in?"

"Sure, you can help me sort these pieces. I'm trying to coordinate the colors and group them into bundles."

"These are t-shirts!" said Phoebe, delighted.

"Yeah, I don't have enough business from Australia and New Zealand yet to keep me busy during our summer, so I'm expanding into a new lightweight line," Jill said. "They're gonna be longer than regular t-shirts, more like tunics or dresses, and have lettuce-edges and asymmetrical hems."

She pointed to one of her dress forms where she had a t-shirt tunic pieced together with pins, "Whaddya think?"

Phoebe went over to get a closer look. "I love it," she said. "How fun, and what a flattering alternative to a boring old t-shirt."

She pulled a fall-colored cardigan off a shelf and held it against herself. "This one would probably sell better in LaLa Land, though."

"That's *Sumac*," said Jill. "And the other one's *Wild Turkey*." Her designs relied on color palettes inspired by Smoky Mountain flora and fauna.

Jill sold a few pieces a week through the boutique in Cloud Forest, the exclusive 5-star dude farm near the park. The world famous resort was called LaLa Land by the locals. It was a lucrative concept – a cleverly reversed version of *The Beverly Hillbillies* where the rich people paid to leave their exclusive gated enclaves for a vacation in the sticks. They could visit *Green Acres* without having to live there.

In a tiny cove that had been a subsistence farm until recently, the urban rich could pay $1,000 a day to sit in rocking chairs and watch other people perform farm labor. It was a canny twist on the venerable Tom Sawyer fence-painting con, but you didn't dare let any of the city people actually touch live animals or farm machinery.

Although they found Cloud Forest absurd, the people of White Oak were grateful for decent jobs close to home. As employees of the fake farm all they had to do was walk around in their regular clothes and talk to each other in their normal speech, while the well-heeled spectators took it all in as part of an elaborate historic reenactment. Although it felt odd to be watched while working in what amounted to a human version of an ant farm, it paid better than the hotels and restaurants in Pigeon Forge and Gatlinburg, and at Cloud Forest they got to work outside in a beautiful place.

Phoebe looked out the large window and saw another flash coming from the same place she'd seen earlier. Jill noticed her worried look and said, "Are you still seein something out there?"

Phoebe nodded, then she said, "It's probably nothin." But she didn't look convinced.

CHAPTER 15

When he had the mother bear and her cubs safely housed at the wildlife building, Henry upended the torn backpack onto his desk. Then he carefully checked each of the separate compartments and emptied them.

He examined every item in the pack, looking for clues. There was nothing to identify the owner, but he did find something interesting. It was a brass key with code numbers stamped into it. The numbers were GSM-147.

It was an official Department of Interior key. The GSM meant Great Smoky Mountains and the numbers identified a particular lock on the roster of buildings under the stewardship of the park. Henry didn't know where lock number 147 was, but he knew somebody who would.

He walked over to the maintenance compound to talk to Jimmy Helton, a machinist and the park key maker.

Henry stuck his head into Jimmy's shop. Jimmy was welding, but shut off his torch and raised his mask when he saw Henry. "Hey Jimmy," Henry said, handing him the key. "Sorry to bother you, but I was wonderin if you could tell me what this is for?"

"Let's see," he said looking at the number stamped into the brass.

"Not off the top of my head, but we have our ways. Follow me."

He led Henry over to his key making department, a tiny, metal-filled cubbyhole, where he used two dirty index fingers to peck at the keys on his computer.

My how park rangering has changed, Henry thought.

"It's to the little lodge up on Laurel Ridge."

Henry tried to picture the place in his mind's eye, but had only the vaguest recollection of it.

"I can understand why he'd want you to have emergency access to it," Jimmy said. "It'd be a tolerable place to hole up in if you got stuck out on the ridge, but I hope he told you it hasn't been repaired yet."

"It hasn't?" said Henry, hoping he sounded like he understood what Jimmy was talking about.

"No, he hasn't scheduled a work detail since he reported it uninhabitable. This is a spare key I made for him, but the cabin is out of service. It's off limits for VIPs or visiting scientists, even for rangers. He asked me take it off the building roster, but I just marked it as inactive."

"Oh," said Henry. He peeked at the screen over Jimmy's shoulder and saw the name associated with the key. It was Fielding, the Park Superintendent.

"I'm sure our fearless leader has more important things on his mind than some old cabin that's fallin in."

"I hear ye," agreed Henry. He thanked Jimmy and left, taking the key with him.

Talk about your rock and a hard place. Henry decided not to

mention the key to anybody else. His priority was to track down the owner of the backpack. Establishing a connection between a shredded backpack, the Superintendent, and a broken down cabin was more than he cared to undertake. He'd have to pursue that part of his investigation discreetly since he stayed in enough trouble with his boss as it was.

Despite his reservations, late in the day, when Henry's tasks took him close to Laurel Ridge Lodge, he decided to swing by and take a look.

The cabin was one of the original buildings left from the days before the park was created when the land was privately owned. He saw why it was referred to as a lodge. This cabin was built in a place so steep, it couldn't have been associated with a farm. It must've been used for camping or hunting or as a family getaway.

From the outside the building appeared to be in good shape. The shake roof and log walls were perfectly intact. He tried the key in the lock and it turned easily, leaving a gray residue on his fingertips. He looked at the stain more closely. It was graphite. Someone had serviced the lock recently.

The door swung back soundlessly on its hinges. The one-room cabin was simply furnished in yuppie rustic. It had a red enamel woodstove for heating and cooking, a small scrubbed pine dinner table, a couple of hickory stick chairs with the bark still on them, a bed made with rope springs and a simple mattress. The flannel sheets and Hudson Bay blanket were from L.L. Bean.

The cabinets in the kitchen area were stocked with coffee, tea, hot chocolate, packets of ramen noodle soup mix, water purification gear, a few dishes and mugs, some flatware, a small assortment of pots and pans, and cooking utensils. Everything was clean and neat. The place wasn't dusty or musty. Someone had to be using it regularly.

Henry searched the room methodically. It wasn't until he got down on his hands and knees to look under the bed, however, that he located a clue to the cabin's occupant. He found a tiny metal pine cone. He examined it carefully. Actually it was a sequoia cone. It was one of the ornaments that decorated a National Park Service hatband.

Over the years, the cones had been made of various metals, the most recent ones being gold-plated. But hatbands could be transferred from one hat to another because the bands tended to last longer than the hats themselves. Occasionally a collector might have an antique band with sterling silver ornaments or a high-ranking park official might even wear a vintage band as a status symbol.

Fielding was a bit of a dandy. He wore a very rare hatband with ornaments made of nickel. The cone Henry held in his hand was also made of nickel. He sighed and sat down in the floor holding the incriminating cone. He rubbed his eyes, as if that would make the thing go away.

He tried to focus on the good news. At least there was no dead body in the cabin, no blood anywhere, and no signs of a struggle. He'd never liked his boss, but he couldn't see the guy murdering anyone. His 72-hour workday just kept getting worse. He tilted his head back against the bed to try and figure out what to do next, but was too tired to formulate a plan. With his eyes closed it took less than a minute for him to drift off to sleep.

CHAPTER 16

Phoebe sat up suddenly, roused from a nightmare with a huge rush of adrenalin. She threw off the light blanket and flopped back down, lying with her arms flung out, bathed in sweat, waiting for the nausea and dizziness to pass.

She dreaded these dreams. She used the front of her shirt to blot the sweat off her face, and tried to recover from the horrible image of the blond-haired girl dangling helplessly in the tree.

Phoebe always tried to look on the bright side of life, but at times like this it was hard to find one. Precognitive dreams were simply a fact of life for the women in her family. She usually didn't know who the person in the dream was or where the scene would be played out, but she could be certain it would happen just the way she saw it.

When the phone rang, she was grateful for the interruption. "Hey girl!" said a loud and perky voice, "What'er ye up to?"

"Takin a nap. What time is it?"

"It's late."

"Then why are you callin? Is Bruce makin you hound people at their homes now?"

"Heck no, you know Bruce can't make me do anything I don't want to. I'm just checkin to be sure you're okay."

At first Phoebe was confused and wondered how Waneeta could possibly know she'd had a bad dream, but then she shook off the fog of sleep and realized it was still the day of her boyfriend's funeral.

"Yeah," Phoebe mumbled, "I'm okay."

"Well, don't worry about anything, honey, if you wanna take some time off I'll find somebody to cover for you."

"You don't have to do that. I'd rather stay busy."

Phoebe'd learned long ago that taking care of other people was the best way to keep her mind off her own problems.

"Well, if that's what ye want," Waneeta said. "I'll be thinkin of ye. Call if ye need anything."

Phoebe thanked her and hung up the phone. She laid on the couch for a few more minutes offering a brief heartfelt prayer for Sean and for the girl she'd seen in her dream. Then she got up and went into the kitchen to make dinner.

The sun was setting as she scrambled a couple of eggs and ate them on thin slices of whole wheat toast. As she chewed she stared longingly at the little gallery of Nikola Tesla photos on the refrigerator.

There was a formal portrait and also a couple of pictures of him at work. They were all in black and white. Tesla had such a handsome face. Phoebe was in love with him.

They'd never met, because he'd died more than a decade before she was born, but she loved him anyway. She stared at the photo of him sitting calmly reading, while beside him an electrical monstrosity threw out sparks and lightning bolts every which way.

To Phoebe's way of thinking Tesla was the perfect man. He was beautiful, brilliant, and geeky. He loved animals and lived off crackers and milk. He could've been the world's first billionaire, but he wouldn't take the time to sign the paperwork because he didn't want to be distracted from his work.

For the similar reasons he'd chosen to be celibate and unmarried. People who didn't understand him said all kinds of goofy things about him, but his work spoke for itself. Some of the most famous scientists and inventors in history had stolen their best stuff from him, Edison for one. Tesla was the guy who was actually responsible for electricity and radio.

Nikola was possibly one of the reasons Phoebe had never married. She didn't dare tell anyone, though. They wouldn't understand. Sometimes she thought she might be in contact with his spirit because whenever she thought of him for more than a few seconds, it made her dizzy and she could see visions of rainbows shaped like doughnuts and other things that didn't actually exist as far as she knew.

Reading the letters of Keats did something similar. She always got the feeling Keats was sitting next to her in bed, reading along with her, and really enjoying himself. Keats was pleasant company, but it seemed like a weird way to live and it wasn't anything she could talk to anyone about.

She took a hot bath with a few drops of spikenard in the water. Spikenard was the essential oil that Mary Magdalene poured over Jesus's head in the incident that set Judas off. Just a couple of drops filled the room with a powerful, complex smell that had a hypnotic, tranquilizing quality. She could only imagine the effect of emptying a whole bottle of it onto someone.

It was the calming aspect that Phoebe needed, although she

naively hoped her trials were behind her. She stayed in the bath for quite a while, adding hot water several times before daring to go back to her bedroom. On the way she searched out a book from her small library.

She climbed into her tall antique iron bed and got under a quilt covered with a pattern of small red roses. She sat propped up by four pillows and began re-reading Rudolf Steiner's matter-of-fact explanation of why some people were able to communicate with the dead and others weren't. And why some people had dreams that would come true the next day.

It made Phoebe feel slightly less crazy to read Steiner's calm descriptions of spiritual matters that might seem odd to people who didn't have experiences like she did. Steiner was no nut. He was a scientist who'd invented a lot of great stuff like reinforced concrete. And he'd written the first books on organic farming and special education for handicapped people. And he'd been a contemporary of Tesla's. She wondered if they knew each other.

When she started having trouble following what she was reading, she closed the book and turned off the light, but still she didn't lay down flat. She sat in the dark, staring, for a long time.

She prayed hard for Sean, for the blond-haired girl in her dream, for Wanda and Mrs. Willard, for Doc and Jill, for Leon and Henry, her parents, and for the whole world.

Sometime in the wee hours of the morning she finally drifted off to sleep.

While Phoebe slept, Ivy Iverson roused again. She could no longer feel her legs at all. She had to get her weight out of the climbing harness because it was acting like a tourniquet on her lower extremities. And she was cold. She needed to get out of the wind. At this altitude, the temperature could drop thirty degrees or more at night and the dampness made the cold even more penetrating.

Climbing was out of the question, as was re-rigging her ropes or anything else that required dexterity, or balance, or clear vision. But lowering herself was possible. All she had to do was press down on the Blake's hitch and it would let her descend in a slow, controlled fashion. She remembered she wouldn't be able to make it to the ground because she was very high in the tree and her ropes weren't long enough. She struggled to focus. She had to be careful and not go down too far or she'd run out of rope and fall the remaining eight stories.

If she could lower herself just enough to reach a limb to sit on, she thought maybe she could survive for a while longer. If she stayed hanging and exposed as she was, she didn't think she'd make it. She marshaled what strength she had left and pressed carefully on the climbing knot. The gentle downward slide made her dizzy and nauseous. She thought she might be about to faint so she let go of the knot. As soon as she stopped applying pressure to the hitch, her descent arrested.

There were no limbs directly below her, so somehow she was going to have to create enough lateral momentum to swing close enough to grab hold of one. That wasn't an easy maneuver when she was in good condition, now it might prove impossible. But she had to try, so, like a small child in a swing whose legs were too short to reach the ground, she thrashed as rhythmically as she could and set herself to rocking.

After long minutes of horrible nausea, she felt something scrape against her left hand and realized she'd touched evergreen needles. She lowered herself a few more inches and continued swinging until she managed to grab some twigs and use that as leverage to get an ankle onto the far side of a branch. Then she twisted and lowered herself until she was sitting astride a large limb with her back to the trunk of the giant hemlock. She scooted until her back was against the tree. Then she used her hands to lift her benumbed legs one at a time until she was sitting supported by the tree trunk with both legs stretched out in front of her.

For safety, she remained tied into her harness and connected to the climbing rope, so that even if she fell off the limb where she was sitting, she wouldn't go far. She lashed her legs loosely to the branch she sat on and used a short auxiliary loop to wrap around a small branch that jutted out beside her. She hoped that would keep her from pitching sideways. Then she went to sleep, or passed out. She was in no condition to tell the difference.

CHAPTER 17

What used to be a dream job, getting paid for hunting, had become a burden for Henry. The hours were terrible and there was no fun in it really. Things weren't done in the old ways anymore. He wasn't a hunter, he was a professional killer and he didn't play fair. A six thousand dollar sound-suppressed sniper rifle and another four thousand for state-of-the-art night vision headgear meant his targets hardly had a chance.

And after a certain point, the pure labor of killing got to be a real drag, literally. You couldn't just kill and be done with it. You had to get rid of the body. Heaving dead weight through heavy undergrowth on such uneven ground was no easy task.

He stepped carefully along the deeply rutted dirt path, placing one foot directly in front of the other. Although he was wearing boots with heavy lugged soles, his footfalls made virtually no sound. The Marines had taught him to walk like that. It was the military version of a model's stalk down the catwalk.

It was 3 a.m. There was only a sliver of a moon. The weak illumination it provided was almost totally obscured by the heavy cloud cover. He'd had the benefit of several hours of darkness for his eyes to adjust. He was always amazed at how well the human eye could see in the dark when there was no artificial light shining anywhere to spoil things.

He didn't need to rely on his own night vision though, because he had some high-tech assistance. An elastic headband held a sophisticated loupe in front of his right eye and provided him with an image so sharp he could make out individual blades of grass on the forest floor. The optical enhancement was so much better than his normal vision, it made him feel like Superman.

He focused his mind until events from earlier in the day were forgotten. The mysterious backpack, the bears, the crowds in Cades Cove, the cabin on Laurel Ridge, and even running into Phoebe McFarland again. All these things were put aside.

Henry heard something moving in the woods off to his right and instantly froze, in effect making himself invisible. Anyone looking his way would've been deceived by the expertly chosen leaves he'd sewn onto his camouflage ghillie suit. It was the latest in *haute couture* for stalkers.

He consciously forced himself to relax his grip on the rifle. The rustling continued, apparently angling toward the trail he was on, whatever it was would intersect the trail several yards ahead of where he was standing.

Moments later something stepped out of the woods and onto the trail in front of him. Henry's hybrid gaze, one mechanical eye and one green eye, met a pair of surprised but shrewd piggy eyes.

The beast was sparsely covered with coarse black hair and sported an impressive set of curved, razor-sharp tusks, called *tushes* in the local language. Wild hogs, or *tush hogs* as they were called, were formidable creatures, pure survival machines. In Smokies dialect critters like this one were called *Rooshins* because they still bore traces of the original stock brought over from Russia.

The fierce Russian hogs had been imported to a private hunting preserve long ago and had either escaped or been intentionally released into the surrounding wilderness. They were astonishingly aggressive animals. Homicidal marathon pigs. Even ones like this, which were the result of interbreeding with feral domestic hogs, had amazing abilities to fight, climb, and navigate the terrain. They had huge shoulders and tiny hindquarters like a Smokies version of a Tasmanian devil. A man would never be able to outrun one.

But Henry was a brave man and an experienced professional hunter. Before the wild hog could gore him, it was dead.

There'd been no loud crack from the rifle, so there was no echo to bounce off the neighboring ridge. The single shot he'd fired made only a popping sound because he was using subsonic ammunition and the rifle was silenced. Considering *who* he was and especially *where* he was, it wouldn't do to make a lot of noise.

He moved down the trail and knelt to make sure the boar was dead. He couldn't leave the carcass where it was. He needed to move it well off the trail where it wouldn't be seen or smelled by hikers.

He slung his rifle across his back and grabbed a trotter. The terrain was steep and rough. It took twenty minutes to drag the body two dozen yards downhill through the dense brush. It was hard work and he was winded. He paused to rest.

He heard a commotion up on the trail and turned to see what it was. He could make out nothing but a shadow with his naked eye, but the night loupe revealed a large black bear standing on the edge of the trail, looking at him, slapping its huge paws hard against the ground. He knew better than to run or climb a tree, so he stood his ground and quickly reviewed his options. The bear huffed and snorted and made gruesome clacking noises with its jaws.

He let go of the pig's foot. In the same instant, the bear started down the hill bounding in a series of great leaps, hooting like a baboon each time it hit the ground. The sight was terrifying, as it was meant to be.

He continued to face toward the bear, but moved off to one side, away from the hog's body, as quickly as he could without appearing to be fleeing. The bear ignored him, snatched up the hog carcass in its jaws, and ran back up the bank with it. It was unbelievable. It took the bear less than a minute to take the hog back to the same place it'd been shot.

He marveled at the bear's strength and at his own luck. Then he made his way back to the trail, taking a wide detour around the bear's impromptu feast. A hundred yards further along the ridge he came to a tent pitched right in the middle of the trail.

He mumbled some choice words when he saw it.

Two backpacks were resting on the ground, leaning against the side of the tent. Light snoring could be heard coming from within. *Eejits*, he thought. It was local dialect for *idiot* handed down from the Gaelic.

He slipped off his night vision headpiece and his ski mask, and stashed them with his rifle behind a tree before approaching the tent. Then he squatted down and said, "Hey in there. You need to wake up."

He heard movement and mumbling from inside.

"It's Henry Matthews. I'm a park ranger," he continued. "Sorry, but you can't camp here, it's illegal. You need to get up right now and move on down to one of the shelters. It's not safe for you to stay here. There's a black bear in the area."

Both the bear and the hog could've been on their way to the tent when he'd intercepted them. How many times and how many different ways could people be told and still not hear? They were risking their lives whenever they failed to secure their food and their packs well away from their tent. Instead these two had actually baited a trap with *themselves.*

Henry waited for the couple to dress, trying not to listen to the grumbling going on inside the tent. Then he spent the next hour escorting them to the closest shelter and showing them how to use the cables to stow their gear up in the air, away from the sleeping area.

As he continued on his regular patrol, he contemplated events of the night. Bears and hogs weren't stupid. They didn't enjoy making life hard for themselves, so if there was a convenient trail, they took it. Seventy-two miles of the Appalachian Trail, known as the AT, ran through the park, following the highest ridgeline in the Smokies. As he walked the trail, his feet straddled the boundary between Tennessee and North Carolina. At night, the narrow rutted track was an interstate for critters through the national park.

He marveled that although he was moving away from a stretch with the highest altitudes in the entire 2,178 mile-long Appalachian Trail, there were no majestic vistas because the path ran through dense forest. Hiking it in the middle of the night like he did, there was even less of a view.

For all the heart-warming imagery built up around being a park ranger he sometimes felt like he was simply a paid poacher. He roamed the most densely trafficked areas, stealthily murdering hairy critters in an effort to hold back the surging tide of wildflower-eating, trail-plowing pigs that were spoiling things for tourists, hikers, and the indigenous plants and animals that had the right to call this place home. The stinking invaders were strong and clever and had endless appetites.

The events of this evening made it clear that he'd killed so many hogs on the AT, to protect clueless hikers like the ones he'd just encountered, that the bears had learned to recognize the sound of his suppressed rifle. He'd created Pavlov's bears. For them, the distinctive muffled crack was now serving as a dinner bell. The bear tonight had gotten to him awfully quick, so they must have started to trail him while he was hunting.

Henry suspected he'd have nightmares about the huge bear hooting and bouncing downhill toward him. He shivered at the thought.

CHAPTER 18

Fall was crunch time for the bears. They turned into eating machines, desperate to consume as many calories as they could so they'd have a good chance to survive the winter sleep and the first few weeks of spring when there weren't many edible plants available. The bears' focus on food meant they were less prone to abandon their eating and run away when they saw people, thus allowing aggressive photographers and other types of idiots to get closer than normal while they were foraging.

Things were a lot more likely to go wrong when people crowded the bears. Because of this, during the fall, Henry worked as close to 24/7 as he could. So after just a few hours of sleep, he resumed his search for the owner of the backpack. He dropped by his subterranean cubbyhole of an office in the National Park Service Headquarters building at The Sugarlands, an impressive stone structure built by the Civilian Conservation Corps in the 1930's. He called around to all the ranger stations and visitor centers to see if anyone had reported an incident with a bear or the loss of a backpack.

There were the usual DUIs, car wrecks, heart attacks, and sprained ankles that had to be dealt with, but nothing had been reported that seemed related to the backpack. Each of the people reported missing on trails during the previous week had been found and returned to their vehicles in good enough condition to drive home on their own. Next, he checked the master schedule of events in the park and saw that nearly a dozen flora and fauna surveys were in full swing. He headed for the Twin Creeks Science and Education Center to see if any of the survey participants were missing or had lost a backpack.

Twin Creeks was the command center for Discover Life in America, DLIA, and its All Taxa Bio-Inventory activities. The building was a striking bit of green architecture built on an open plan, with gigantic wooden beams cut from trees harvested from the building site, a foundation of rounded stones gathered from a creek that ran alongside the building, glass walls, and plenty of skylights.

He arrived during the morning briefing before the forayers, questers, and blitzers dispersed into the field for the day's work. Henry politely interrupted the speaker and held up the ominously shredded backpack. "I'm trying to find the owner of this backpack. Do any of you recognize it?"

Several people came forward for a closer look. Two men were especially intense in their examination. The younger of them said, "I think I know who this belongs to. This purple is pretty distinctive. I think its Ivy's. Ivy Iverson's."

"What's your name?" Henry asked.

"Tim Cardwell."

"How do you know Ivy?"

"She's my girlfriend," Tim said, and then he shot an angry look toward the man standing next to him and said, "My *ex*-girlfriend."

"Are you from this area?" Henry asked, noting the man's orange and white t-shirt.

"Yeah, I'm a Ph.D. candidate at U.T. in bryophyta."

"What's that?" Henry asked.

"Mosses and liverworts."

"What can you tell me about Ivy?"

"She's at U.T., too. In mycology."

"Do you know how she might've lost her pack?"

Cardwell shook his head. "I haven't been in touch with her recently." He shot the other man another hard look as he said it. "Where'd you find it?"

"Cades Cove," Henry said. "Does she go there a lot?"

"No," said Cardwell, "never. The trees there aren't the kind she's interested in."

"What kind of trees is she interested in?" Henry asked.

"Big ones," said Cardwell. "The tallest ones she can find. She climbs for fun, and for research."

Cardwell looked at the ripped pack with growing dismay and asked, "Did a bear do this?"

"Probably," Henry said, "most of it anyway."

"Did the bear hurt Ivy?"

"I don't know," Henry replied. "That's what I'm trying to find out. We haven't located her yet. Do you have any contact numbers for her?"

Cardwell nodded and then gave Henry Ivy's home and cell numbers. Henry immediately dialed her home, got no answer, and left a brief message asking Ivy to call him as soon as she got his message. He repeated the process with her cell number.

"Is she participating in any of the DLIA surveys?"

Cardwell shook his head. "She didn't even sign up for the Myxo Madness event, and that's her field of study. I checked and she wasn't on the list. That doesn't make any sense. Nothing she does lately makes any sense to me. But even if she wasn't going to the myxo event, she was probably in the park yesterday, somewhere, climbing."

"Any idea where?" Henry asked.

"No, like I said, I haven't talked to her in awhile."

Henry took down a description of Ivy: 24 years old, 5' 8", green eyes, straight blond hair.

"If you hear from her," Henry said, "please let me know right away. Okay?"

Cardwell nodded and took Henry's card.

"And you sir?" Henry asked the other man.

"Alexandre Molyneaux," he said, then spelled both names for Henry, using the French pronunciation for the letters of the alphabet, which meant he had to repeat himself several times.

Cardwell took a last look at the mangled backpack, then turned to go, shoving past Molyneaux with unnecessary force.

Henry looked at Molyneaux with a questioning look.

"He is young," Molyneaux said, dismissively. "This bag, it belong to Ivy. This," he said wiggling a stub of black plastic dangling from a carabiner clipped to the pack, "it is part of a lighted magnifying tool that I give to her. The glass is missing now. It has been broken."

"Do you have any idea where she is?

Molyneaux shook his head.

"Any idea where she was yesterday?"

"I, too, believe she may have been climbing in this park. These trees of majesty in the Smokies are the reason she chose this place for her studies instead of her home state of New Mexico. Such trees do not grow in this desert. But I do not know where she was climbing."

"Do you study the same thing as Ivy?" asked Henry.

"No, I study the butterflies," he said. "I am Professeur au Département de Biologique at Université de Loire. La Société Geographique Francaise pays for my visit in this place."

"How do you know Ivy," Henry asked.

"She enjoys to look at my butterflies," he said smiling. "We have friendliness. That is all."

Henry took down Molyneaux's contact information, gave him a card, and thanked him.

It looked to Henry like Cardwell was a jilted boyfriend who was jealous of whatever was going on between Ivy and the Frenchman, if anything. Henry wasn't sure he believed in a friendship based on mutual appreciation of butterflies either.

Before he left, Henry moved to the middle of the room and addressed the group again. "Excuse me," Henry called out in a loud voice, "I need to ask you all a couple of questions. It'll just take a minute."

The chatter subsided and people turned toward him to see what he wanted.

"Have any of you seen Ivy Iverson recently?"

There was a low buzz in the room, but no one spoke up.

"Please keep your eyes peeled. If anybody sees her or hears from her, please let me or any of the park rangers know immediately. It may be nothing, but we're just being cautious in case she might be out there somewhere in need of assistance."

Henry looked around at the group to get an idea of what kind of people they were. They divided fairly evenly between male and female. Most of them were very fit, tan, many of them were sporting scratches, cuts, and bruises consistent with a struggle. But that didn't necessarily mean anything. The terrain in the park was very rough.

Next Henry made his way to the administrative offices near the center of the building. He explained the problem to Janet Stevens, a ranger and Chief Biologist for the park, and she made him a copy of the roster of participants and maps indicating where the various surveys were taking place.

Henry scanned the list of activities, and asked. "So yesterday and the day before a lot of these people were out in the park?"

Janet nodded, "A couple of hundred volunteers and about a dozen leaders."

"Anybody come back hurt?"

"Sure, the usual stuff, sprains, that sort of thing, but nothing serious that I know of."

"Anybody missing?"

"Nope."

"Anybody report seeing anything unusual?"

"No. Just some tourist stuff about seeing coyotes and thinking they're wolves, and a guy who saw Sasquatch. The Sasquatch guy calls about once a week."

Henry smiled at that. A big bear standing on its hind legs could make anyone think they'd seen Sasquatch. "Well, let me know if you hear anything, okay?"

On his way out Henry walked past an area where Molyneaux had set up a table and was showing something to several young people. Henry glanced at the specimens. They looked like brown bits of dust. Molyneaux looked up and gestured for him to come closer.

"These don't look like any butterflies I ever saw," Henry joked.

"Oh, but you must let me show you. My work is with these smallest of the butterflies."

"Dr. Molyneaux is a nanolepidopterist," one of the volunteers said. "He's a world famous expert in tiny butterflies."

"Would you like to see them?" Molyneaux asked Henry. "Please, look."

Molyneaux gestured toward the stereoscopic microscope. Henry bent and stared through the eyepieces and was astonished. What looked like boring bits of brown lint to the naked eye were absolutely stunning, extremely colorful, under magnification and with illumination from the bright specimen light.

"They're like hummingbirds, aren't they?" Henry asks. "The colors, the way you can see em if the light's right, but other times they don't look like much at all."

"Exactly," says Molyneaux. "Nature can be sometimes shy. She does not easily reveal her secrets. We must be patient, then she will show us her true beauty."

Henry nodded his agreement.

In the last room on the right before he reached the door, Henry saw a woman scientist take a giant bug out of a refrigerator. He stopped to watch what she was doing with it. He was startled to see her place it on the glass of what looked like a fancy copy machine and proceed to Xerox the huge insect. He stood in the hall and watched her repeat the process several times with other gigantic bugs. She'd take them out of the fridge, copy them, and then put them back.

"Excuse me," Henry said, leaning in through the open door. "I was just wonderin, why you're copyin bugs? And how come you keep em in the 'frigerator?"

"I'm scanning beetles for our inventory," she said. "We use this special biological scanner with a high depth of field to capture images of each specimen. I have to keep them cold or they crawl off the scanner."

"They're still alive?" Henry said, surprised.

"Oh yes. See these pincers?" she said, holding the bug so he could see its menacing jaws, "These really hurt, so I keep the beetles refrigerated. The cold puts them into a stupor so they can't bite me."

To be polite, Henry nodded with an understanding he didn't really feel, and then walked away. He understood that people liked to study things, and he didn't want anyone to get bitten, but he wondered how long insects could survive like that. He shivered at the creepiness of condemning any creature, even a bug, to a limbo of eternal cold.

CHAPTER 19

Sometimes Phoebe saw patients who were not going to get well.

Her first call of the morning was on Mrs. Willard, a lady in the last stages of pancreatic cancer who didn't want to die in the hospital. She wanted to live out her last days at home in the same house where she'd been born 93 years before. She was bedridden but was fortunate to have a nice family who were taking good care of her. There wasn't much Phoebe could do, but she knew it was a comfort to the family if a professional nurse came by every so often to see how things were going.

Phoebe considered it an honor to attend to people at the end of their lives. She was deeply impressed with the grace and courage people demonstrated when their options were exhausted. Mrs. Willard was an interesting lady. She was tiny, barely five feet tall, with a fluffy halo of snow white curls. A kind disposition and good humor radiated from her despite her illness.

Phoebe bathed her thoroughly and carefully with a washcloth and basin, always keeping an eye out for pressure sores or any rashes, but there were none. She applied lotion to Mrs. Willard's skin, and added a little bit of rose oil to suffuse the room with a pleasant, peaceful scent. Phoebe gently rolled her first to one side, then to the other, as she put on fresh sheets in the clever way nurses had of changing a bed with someone in it.

She plumped and adjusted the pillows to get her patient as comfortable as possible, then sat on the edge of the bed to chat. Mrs. Willard wanted to know all the most recent local developments and Phoebe entertained her with cheerful gossip.

"This is such a nice room," Phoebe said. "You can lay in bed and see that pretty maple tree out the window."

"This was the girls' room when I was little. Many's the year my sisters and me've laid up in this bed and looked out on that tree. I wasn't even born whenever Grandaddy planted it. I'm glad it'll outlast us all."

Phoebe smiled.

"I lived here til I was fifteen. Then, when I got married, I moved out to live with Joe in a little cabin over near Cosby, where the park is now. The cabin's probably long gone by now. I heard the government lets em fall in cause they don't want people stayin in em."

Phoebe nodded.

"My children were born in that cabin. Eight of em. I've outlived em all and my husband, my friends. I've even outlived one of my grandchildren. It's strange when nobody's left who remembers the same things I remember. Nobody but me's alive on this earth to remember Momma and Daddy. They wouldn't believe the things that's happened. They saw some changes during their lives, but not like the ones I've seen.

"Everthing seems to be gettin speeded up all the time, don't it? You think things can't get any more expensive or go any faster, but they keep on doin it."

Phoebe murmured agreement.

"I've had a real good life and I thank God for it all, the good and the bad, but I'm ready. I'm not a bit sad or worried about what's comin next. I'm lookin forward to it. Almost everbody who's important to me's on the other side, a waitin for me. I've made em wait a long time, too."

"I thank you for comin," she said and took hold of one of Phoebe's hands. She held it in both of hers for a few moments, then she bent and kissed it in a gesture so sweet it made tears come to Phoebe's eyes. Phoebe bent and kissed her on the forehead and said softly, "God bless you."

Both women knew they'd never see each other again in this life.

As she drove away Phoebe thought about the difference in a death that was natural and expected and Sean's death, which was neither.

And she wondered about the girl in her dream. Could there be a connection between the girl and Sean? If there was some connection, why hadn't she dreamed about Sean, too? She hadn't been able to help her boyfriend, but maybe she was meant to help the girl somehow.

CHAPTER 20

Henry made several calls to the University of Tennessee before he was able to track down the person who was overseeing Ivy Iverson's doctoral studies. It was Professor Conrad T. Whittington, a botanist who the department secretary said couldn't take his call because he was away from the office. In fact, she said, he was inside the national park supervising a Fern Foray.

Henry called DLIA to get the exact location of the foray, then drove out to Big Creek to talk to the professor. He had to hike nearly a mile along a trail that ran through a lush fairyland of curling green fronds. Then he caught up with a group of about a dozen people who were in and slightly off the trail thrashing about in a thicket of briars. They seemed to be searching for something. "Is this it?" one of them called out.

A large man crashed through the heavy undergrowth, squatted down, and disappeared for a few moments. Then he stood up and said, "No, this has opposing leaflets, a Christmas fern has alternating leaflets."

The group stopped what they were doing and clustered around him. The teacher was over six feet tall and heavy, with muscle that was turning to fat in middle age. He was touching the plant gently as he explained something about spores.

He looked up when Henry approached and smiled in a near-sighted, distracted way. "Let the gentleman pass," he told the forayers. "Please forgive us," he said to Henry, "we're dallying."

"Can I watch?" Henry said.

"Of course," said Whittington, and he turned back to the plant saying, "as you can see …" He was interrupted by a woman calling out, "Oh yuck, what's that?"

The Professor turned to see what she was looking at. "It's a type of fungus," he said. "The Latin name is *Xylaria polymorpha.* The common name is *Dead Man's Fingers.*"

"Good name for it," the woman said. "It's disgusting."

The Professor went back to his lecture about the fern without seeming to mind the interruption. When he finished, the group, most of whom were scratched and bug-bitten from their efforts, continued along the trail. Henry said, "Professor Whittington, can I talk to you a minute?"

"Certainly," Whittington said. "Do you mind walking with me? I dare not take my eyes off the group for fear of what they might get up to."

"I hear ye," Henry said, and fell into step just behind and slightly to the left of the big man because the trail wasn't wide enough to walk alongside him. I wanted to ask you a couple of questions about a student of yours, Ivy Iverson."

"Ivy Iverson," Whittington mumbled to himself, trying to place her, "Ivy Iverson … oh yes … I'm acquainted with the young lady to whom you refer. Has Miss Iverson done something she shouldn't have?"

"I'm not sure," Henry said. "Right now, it looks like she might've gone missing. I'm trying to locate her. You don't happen to have any idea where she is, do you?"

"Me?" Whittington said, "No. I wish I could be of assistance. I certainly hope she's alright, but unfortunately I have very little contact with Miss Iverson."

"I thought you were her major professor," Henry said.

"I am," Whittington said, "but … are we off the record here?"

Henry nodded.

"Miss Iverson is not the most devoted scholar I've ever supervised."

He called out to the group of adults, saying, "Stay together! Don't venture too far ahead please!" He turned back to Henry and said, "It's fairly obvious to anyone who is acquainted with her, that Miss Iverson enrolled at the University of Tennessee in order to have access to the trees in this park. She likes to climb them you see.

"Many students choose universities with an eye toward proximity to the Smokies, the Rockies, the beach, or winter sports rather than for academic reasons. Miss Iverson seems a decent sort, but unfortunately she's rather immature, and not a particularly promising scientist."

Henry tilted his head, appraising Whittington.

"Sorry I can't be of more help, but I simply don't know the girl well enough. Perhaps it's a failing in my tutelage that I've not insisted she maintain better contact."

"Professor! Professor!" someone called out. "What's this, *Dead Man's Toes*?"

The question drew snickers from the group. The professor

looked toward the forayers, torn between his questioners. Henry knew he'd better wrap it up. "Do you know what she was working on?"

"No, I'm afraid I don't. She has not stated the direction of her research formally, nor even decided on anything informally, as far as I'm aware."

"Any idea what area of the park she favored for her research?"

He shook his head, then he looked at Henry in a distracted way, saying, "I'm so sorry. You must forgive me, but I need to resume the foray before any of my volunteers wander off to parts unknown."

Whittington lumbered away, moving along the trail in a bear-like, side-to-side waddle. Henry remembered that the technical term for that gait was *plantigrade* and was pleased that he'd remembered some of his college biology lessons. He followed the Professor with his eyes for a few moments, then turned to hike back to his vehicle. He'd walked only a few minutes when he was passed by a vigorous elderly lady wearing a t-shirt emblazoned with the slogan *Non Impediti Ratione Congitatonis*.

Henry smiled and greeted her as all rangers do when encountering another person on a trail. Then he asked, "What's the sayin on your shirt mean?"

"It's Latin," she said, "It means *Unencumbered by the Thought Process.*"

Then the woman, who had to be in her seventies if not eighties, clambered up the steep hillside next to the trail with the agility of a mountain goat and was out of sight a couple of seconds later.

The exchange was so other-worldly, Henry wondered if it was real. He'd had a series of strange encounters in the park in the last couple of days. He tried to shake off the feeling of discombobulation by walking back to his truck as fast as possible.

CHAPTER 21

Phoebe pondered death and dreams as she drove away from Mrs. Willard's house and toward her next call. When her phone chirped to let her know she had a message, it startled her out of her meditative state.

She played the message. "Hey Phoebe, it's Henry. It looks like I'll be goin to Cataloochee to change out that elk's collar this afternoon. I'z wonderin if you might still wanna come along. You'll like it. It's a real pretty area."

"Oh, and I found out who that backpack belonged to, but I can't get in touch with the owner, so I need to keep tryin to track em down in case somethin's gone wrong. They coulda got hurt or somethin. I doubt any of our bears would've hurt em, but you never know. Bears are like people, they all got different personalities. If you run into the wrong bear on the wrong day …. Well anyway, let me know if you'd like to go." Then he gave her a number to call.

Henry was such a good person. Phoebe didn't have a single bad memory of him. Of course, nearly all her memories of him were more than half a lifetime ago. But still, she hoped they could be friends again like they'd been when they were little. She could use a friend.

She thought about the invitation, but she was torn. She wanted to see Cataloochee and the elk, and even Henry. But the Henry she'd been friends with had been young. Now he was a man.

Phoebe didn't want any more man problems. She wasn't in any condition to go through more of that. In fact, she was pretty sure she didn't want to go on another date for the rest of her life. She liked men, but at this point she didn't really want one in her house. She knew she was getting set in her ways, but she enjoyed directing her own life.

So, she decided to give the trip a pass and continued toward her next house call. A few minutes later, though, as she thought about the mystery of the backpack, she realized Henry hadn't told her who it belonged to. In the end, curiosity won out and she returned Henry's call and arranged to meet him later in the day.

Phoebe made a stop at the gas station that was used as an office by White Oak's redneck mafia. It was a charming old Esso station that Lester and Fate had spared no expense in restoring to glittering original condition.

Sitting around a table in a vintage booth from a diner surrounded by Sinclair Dino and Tony Tiger memorabilia, the low key duo oversaw all the illegal, surreptitious, and questionable activities in the area, including most of the professional plant and animal poaching, illegal drug and alcohol production, thieving, and goodness knew what else.

Times were changing in East Tennessee. Law enforcement's tentacles could reach nearly everywhere nowadays – everywhere but a place that enjoyed the isolation and insularity of the Smokies.

In White Oak any stranger would be immediately obvious and locals weren't likely to tell a stranger anything. Cell phones and computers were useless in most of the area. The dense vegetation and cave-riddled rock made many kinds of aerial surveillance ineffective, as Eric Rudolf had demonstrated to the intense frustration of national law enforcement authorities.

A place like this was in great demand by criminals of all stripes. That meant the men's connections were no longer merely local, but extended into organized crime both in the U.S. and overseas. In this new market, white trash could trade up. Lester and Fate's kids could be the next Kennedy or Rockefeller.

Criminal dynasties fascinated Phoebe. America was run by them, and as far as Phoebe knew, so was every other country in the world. The most successful ones hid not only in plain sight, but in the Presidency, Capitol Hill, and as CEOs of all the biggest companies.

She'd never thought much about badness in a bloodline til a friend who worked at Child Protective Services said they'd done a survey and found that nearly every serious case of child abuse or neglect in Knoxville involved one of seven local families. So, crime, like a lot of other things, ran in families.

As Phoebe walked through the door, Steve Earle's redneck anthem, *Copperhead Road*, was playing from a beautiful antique jukebox. The eerie wailing of bagpipes, manic Irish fiddle, and percussion at the emphatic but constrained pace of clogging perfectly conveyed the raucous and relentless mood of the mountain culture.

Fate pointed a remote control toward the jukebox and the volume was reduced to a faint background noise. Polite greetings were exchanged. Not for the first time, Phoebe marveled at the lovely manners you so often encountered in sociopaths, at least the ones you got along with.

"To what do we owe this pleasure?" asked Lester, pronouncing the last word *play-zure,* then spitting tobacco into a container at his feet. At least Phoebe hoped there was a container there. He was a huge man with hands big enough to palm Phoebe's whole head.

He was wearing a vintage green work shirt with the name *Bob* embroidered in an oval patch on the left chest. For a moment Phoebe wondered if it was some sort of hillbilly alias, Lester, AKA, *Bob.* But then she realized it was simply more of the gas station memorabilia.

"I just wanted to thank you gentlemen for the antibiotics. I really appreciate em. Your kindness will help a lot of people around here who can't afford the high-dollar medicine. Might even save some lives."

The men looked at each other with feigned confusion.

They were good, Phoebe thought to herself. Real pros. But if you knew who they were, the performance seemed more like a skit in the Redneck Crooks Comedy Tour.

"Well, thanks anyway," she said and started to leave, then remembered Henry saying he couldn't get hold of the owner of the backpack. Maybe these guys would know something that would help. She knew they'd never tell her anything straight out, but she also knew she'd be able to tell if they actually did know anything from the way they answered her.

She turned back and said, "I'd don't mean to bother ya'll, but it looks like somebody mighta gone missin in the park. I'z wonderin if y'all'd seen or heard anything about that."

Both men shook their heads with expressions that said they were terribly sorry not to be able to be of assistance, but they just didn't know a thing about it. Seeing this pantomime performed *à deux,*

Phoebe realized it was an expression that men in their lines of work would've had to perfect early in their careers.

Engaging in the occasional brief conversation with them was one thing, but Lester and Fate had reputations for being *mean*, which, in the Smokies and depending on who was talking, covered anything from rudeness up to and including serial killing. Phoebe wasn't exactly scared of these men, but something in their manner made her wonder if the missing backpacker might've accidentally stumbled onto something they shouldn't have. And maybe Sean had, too.

If these guys didn't want a body to be found, it wouldn't be. Thugs in the Smokies didn't fool around with sissy drive-by shootings or botched disposals of ashes. They were highly effective killers, trained from childhood to hunt, shoot, and everything that went along with that. It was why most of the military snipers were recruited from the southern Appalachian highlands. Heck, Phoebe could shoot better than most law enforcement or even military personnel. It was just part of the local culture.

"Well, I sure would appreciate it if you'd let me know if you do happen to hear anything."

"We sure will," said Fate.

Phoebe wasn't certain, but she suspected both of them were struggling to hide smiles.

CHAPTER 22

"Where are ye?" said Waneeta.

"Just leavin the Esso station. Went by to talk to the guys."

"Why? Did yer car git stole?"

Phoebe laughed. "No, I went to ask em for a favor." She didn't dare mention the drug theft, even to Waneeta.

"You want em to steal ye a new car? God knows you need one. What're ye gonna git?"

"No, I'm not gittin a new car!" said Phoebe, laughing even harder. "And don't you talk bad about my car. Me and Eleanor are doin just fine. We understand each other."

"Okay," said Waneeta in a huff, "Then don't tell me what you're doin consortin with the hillbilly mob."

"I was gonna tell ye, ye just kept interrupting me! I'z tryin to help Henry. He's lookin for somebody who mighta gone missin in the park, so I asked em if they knew anything."

"Think they'd tell ye if they did?"

"Not straight out and certainly not in front of each other, but yeah, one way or another, they'd tell me what they could."

"Those two are scary. They'd cut yer heart out for a nickel."

"I know they've done some bad things, and thank God I don't know exactly what, but honestly, they've always been good to me. I'm not afraid of em. They got a code they go by and I can sorta understand what it is. They're not *crazy*."

"It's funny," said Waneeta, "we can find a way to get along with the criminals we know, but we want the other ones locked up."

"Nobody's all good or all bad. People aren't that simple," said Phoebe. "That's the thing I love about White Oak. Everybody's got their place in the community. Nobody gits left out."

"Nobody except the whole rest of the world!" Waneeta crowed.

"If you can still remember," Phoebe said, "would you mind tellin me why you called?"

"Oh, I almost forgot," said Waneeta. "It's Nerve. She's bein a real pill today. "The family's askin for ye. Accordin to the daughter, you're the only one left Nerve'll recognize. That says loads, don't it?"

Minerva Langston, called Nerve by everyone who knew her, was suffering from dementia. She'd never been easy to deal with, thus her nickname. And if a vote had been held she'd have been voted by the whole community to be the person most likely to go senile in a way that would make her even more cranky.

"Doc always says when people get old, especially if they get senile, they just become *more* of whatever they've always been." She didn't add that he'd told her that when she'd asked him about an old man she saw beating his elderly wife with an aluminum quad-cane in front of the grocery store.

A bystander had intervened before the old coot could kill her, but Phoebe'd always worried about what went on at home when nobody was there to help the woman. She hoped the old lady had put a cast iron skillet upside that mean old man's head.

"Nerve's no problem," said Phoebe. "I'm not far from there."

Phoebe found Nerve interesting. She was crazy and mean, but Phoebe still loved to talk to her because she'd come out with some of the most fascinating things sandwiched in with the ranting. It was like the devil and the angels were at war in her head and if you listened to her, you could hear both sides. Like a radio tuned to the Apocalypse.

When Phoebe got to the house, Nerve's oppressed daughter-in-law, Teresa, nearly collapsed with relief and gratitude. Phoebe hugged her and asked how things were going. She learned that Nerve was refusing food and medicine, staying up day and night, ranting, and accusing everyone of trying to poison her. "Give me a few minutes," Phoebe said, "Then bring her food in. I'll try to git her to eat and take her meds."

She went down the hall to Nerve's room. It was easy to tell where she was because she was shouting in a harsh nasal twang, "Who the hell's that? Whoever it is, tell em go to blazes. They can git the hell outta my house. I don't give a damn who it is."

"Hey there Miss Minnie," Phoebe said, coming into the bedroom where Nerve sat in a rocking chair next to the window. "Hope it's not a bad time. I was missin ye and thought I'd come by for a visit."

Nerve instantly quieted when she heard Phoebe's voice. She held out a gnarled hand to her. Phoebe took it and pulled a beautiful old cane-bottom chair over to sit beside her. They sat like that in silence for several minutes til Phoebe could feel Minerva relax.

Teresa crept into the room and set a tray on the bed. She slid it close enough for Phoebe to reach. "This is some pretty good lookin vegetable soup, Miss Minnie, whaddya say?"

Nerve, it seemed, had run down. She had nothing at all to say. She let Phoebe feed her like a small child and then took her medicine. "Do ye think you might be able to rest now?" Phoebe asked.

Nerve closed her eyes and leaned her head back against the high-backed rocker. Phoebe waited, hoping Minerva'd be able to drop off to sleep. As she sat there, her mind wandered to her grief over Sean's death and then to her sadness over never being able to make her relationships last.

Without opening her eyes, Nerve spoke in a soft voice, saying, "Honey, they's only one kinda woman who's a lookin fer a husband … and that's one who ain't never had one before."

CHAPTER 23

Jill was cleaning the restaurant when she glanced out the window and saw another flash. Any sign of human in an area like that, particularly prolonged signs in the same place were so unusual she decided to take a walk around Greenbrier to see if she could get a better look.

Like most people from the area, Jill loved the mountains. She'd knew she'd never be able to be happy living anywhere else. And she wasn't afraid of the woods. She'd spent her whole childhood and youth roaming around by herself or with friends, building little cabins out of sticks and carpeting them with moss.

She felt safer in the woods than she did a city. The forest was so peaceful. So beautiful.

Jill drove as close to Laurel Mountain as she could, then got out to walk the rest of the way. There was an old logging track that sidehilled, ran parallel to but below the ridgeline. She made her way downhill through the woods, knowing she'd intersect it eventually.

She walked a few minutes until she heard a faint sound like wind chimes, but it was gone before she could be certain she wasn't imagining it.

Moments later, she stepped down onto the old track worn

smooth by mules pulling wooden sleds loaded with lumber. The trail wasn't maintained, so it wasn't easy to travel along it, but it kept to a gentle grade that hugged the side of the hill.

She heard the tinkling sound again. She was sure of it this time. The track was leading her toward it.

The tinkling grew louder. She walked til it was coming from somewhere above her. The footing was uneven, so she walked a few steps, then stopped and scanned the canopy overhead, listening, then walked a few more steps and scanned again.

She could tell she was zeroing in on the source of the sound. She prayed for a moment that the Lord would show her whatever He needed her to see, then she looked up again.

During the lunch hour, Phoebe called her office.

"Hidey there sister, it's Phoebe. Anything goin on?"

"Nothing you'd wanna know about," said Waneeta. "Remember what the politicians say, it's all about plausible deniability."

Both women laughed heartily at Waneeta's wit.

At the sound of Waneeta's rowdy laughter, Bruce heaved himself out of his chair and came to stand in the threshold of his office. He was hesitant to encroach on Waneeta's physical space, but his obvious eavesdropping provoked Waneeta to issue one of her trademark *non sequiturs*, asking Phoebe, "Is the blood bright red, or is it black?"

"Are you on a personal call?" Bruce asked, with narrowed eyes.

Waneeta kept the phone to her ear and shook her head. Bruce

didn't move. Okay, she'd have to ramp it up to get rid of him. Speaking as if trying to reassure a frightened patient, she said, "Honey, they's all kinds of reasons you might be seein blood in the toilet."

Her verbal gambit had the desired effect, Bruce ducked back into his office, but he left the door ajar. In case he was still spying on her conversation, Waneeta added, "Is the blood mixed right in with the stool or is it just floatin out by itself in the toilet water?"

At that Bruce's door slammed.

"How's things goin with that cute ranger?" Waneeta said, as if they'd never been interrupted. "I heard he's single."

"I ain't lookin to git married and anyway, he's married to his job, or so I've been told," said Phoebe.

"You two are pitiful. Just pitiful."

"I'll be perfectly happy to find a kind fella to be friends with. That's all I'm lookin for these days. I am *over* romance."

Waneeta let out a huge sigh.

"A lot of marriageable women don't wanna get married," said Phoebe.

"Name *one*."

"Queen Elizabeth I, Greta Garbo, Coco Chanel. None of them would've had a bit of trouble findin a husband."

"Doris Day got married four times," said Waneeta, "Cleopatra was married four times, twice to her own brothers. And then there's Elizabeth Taylor."

Phoebe was momentarily confused, thinking Cleopatra *was*

Elizabeth Taylor. She didn't want Waneeta to get away with double counting. "Haven't you ever wanted to give up?"

"Oh, *hell* no!" Waneeta said, laughing. "You fall off the horse, you gotta git right back on or else ye might lose yer nerve. Men can smell fear, honey, you can't let em git the upper hand."

"I thought it was horses that could smell fear, or maybe animals in general."

"Men *is* animals," Waneeta said. Over Phoebe's *laughter* she added, "I'm *serious*."

"I ain't getting married!"

"Oh well, marriage ain't always what it's cracked up to be. Or divorces neither."

"You get more work out of your ex-husbands than most women get out of men they're still married to."

"That's true. Jimmy's a great cook. Lately he's been cookin everything off Dale Jr.'s website."

Phoebe tried to imagine Dale Earnhart Jr. cooking and wondered what NASCAR cuisine might be. She visualized frying bacon on an engine block, or a drive thru for cars going over a hundred miles an hour. Her thoughts were interrupted by Waneeta saying, "Carl can fix anything. He's a genius with cars, plumbing, electrical. And Wayne's the best babysitter you could ask for. But it ain't all been a bed of roses, I'm telling ye. I went through a rough time after my second divorce. I hadn't ever told anybody this story cause I was too ashamed, but I'll tell you.

"It was bad enough to find out Wayne was cheatin on me with a woman who had the same name as me. Prob'ly the only way the *eejit* could be sure he wouldn't mess up and call one of us the wrong name! Wayne is *not* a smart man."

Phoebe laughed so hard she dropped the phone. By the time she had it back against her ear, she'd missed part of the story. Waneeta was saying, "… had to find a place of my own and I didn't have no money. The best I could do was rent a used single-wide trailer. I'd always swore to myself that I wouldn't ever live in no trailer, but there I was. I was feelin mighty low.

"The first time I went inside the thing I was dreadin what I'd find. But it turned out to be a nice little place and was as clean as a whistle. In that whole house, there was just one single item left behind by whoever'd lived there before.

"A weddin dress was hangin in a bag in the bedroom closet. Either it'd never been worn or had just come back from the cleaners. Whichever it was, the dress was in absolutely *perfect* condition.

"That dress turned out to be such a blessin. The mystery of tryin to figure out who left it behind, and why, gave me somethin to think about besides myself and my own problems.

"I never did find out whose dress it was or what'd happened to em, but I figured it was a woman who'd lived there before me and she was leavin me a present to show me there was a good future for me out there somewhere. And that, just like her, I wouldn't always be livin there. It was like we was friends, but we never did meet.

"And that woman was right. Before long I was able to move out."

"What a wonderful story," Phoebe said, enchanted. "It's like you were helped by an angel. An angel in a trailer."

"That trailer angel saved me some money, too," said Waneeta

"How?"

"I wore the dress for my third weddin!"

As soon as she hung up, Phoebe reached for the dog-eared spiral notebook she kept beside her seat. It was full of possible lyrics to country music songs. Her secret dream was to write a song for Tim McGraw. And Waneeta's life was a constant source of great material.

She scribbled notes about the pristine wedding dress left behind in a trailer by some unknown person for a broken-hearted woman to find.

Maybe the woman who'd left it had been broken-hearted, too. What an interesting riddle. Just like Waneeta, Phoebe loved a mystery.

CHAPTER 24

When Jill looked up she saw a flash of metal glinting in the sun and a patch of yellow. It looked like a piece of cloth. She moved a few steps to get a better view. It was a jacket worn by someone perched high up in a tree. They were sitting on a limb with their back against the trunk and their legs stretched out in front of them.

Whoever it was had colorful ropes running up into the tree above where they were sitting and also dangling down below them. There were bits of metal hitting against each other and jingling as the ropes blew in the breeze. This was the source of the tinkling sounds and the glinting.

Jill called out to the climber, but got no response. She moved around and parted the foliage to get a better look. The blond hair cascading around the slumped head made her think it was a woman. She called several more times, then finally she saw the person try to raise their head. One of their hands twitched and fell to the side, but that was all.

Clearly something was wrong. Jill needed to get help, but there was no cell service in the area. And there was no way for Jill to get to the woman or get her down by herself. She had no equipment and no climbing skills.

Jill had a strong impulse to hurry back to her car, but she made herself slow down and find a way to mark the place before she left. She looked around for something to use as a flag and for clues as to the climber's identity.

But there was nothing. Absolutely nothing.

Jill knew that animals would carry away food or anything with an interesting smell, but it made no sense that every last bit of the climber's gear would be gone.

Surely the woman had brought more with her than she'd taken up into the tree. But who would've taken her things and left without calling for help once they got to the road? She knew approximately how long the woman had been up there because the flashing had started a day and a half ago.

This was highly suspicious. Maybe it wasn't an accident. Maybe someone had hurt the woman on purpose. But who was it, how had they done it, and why?

Jill walked in a spiral around the base of the tree, widening her search. Then she saw it, a broken stick with a rubber knob on one end. She picked it up. The rubber tip had blood on it. She had no idea what the item was, but she suspected it had been used somehow to hurt the climber. She made a few more widening circuits of the tree, finding nothing, and then changed her mind about how best to help the woman.

She took off her jacket and tied it around a nearby sapling. Her gut told her the quickest and smartest way to get help was to walk to Leon's. The log road would take her most of the way. And walking downhill straight toward Leon's cabin would be faster than hiking back up to her car and driving out via the circuitous route she'd have to take.

Leon lived on his family's farm adjacent to the park. He'd had search and rescue and emergency medical training from the Park Service when he was a teenager. He also had experience recovering lost hikers as a volunteer. And he taught the Boy Scouts how to tie knots and how to climb and rappel. Leon would know what to do and he'd be discreet.

Jill was worried for the woman and wondered what had happened to her. But she wanted to wait til she understood for sure what the situation was before deciding how best to approach the authorities. The people of White Oak preferred to handle local matters among themselves.

Over a thousand local families had been thrown off their land in the 30's to create the park and the feds has sent an arrogant gang of outsiders in to run the place like an occupying army. The locals had seventy-five years worth of reasons to dislike and distrust the invaders. There was no rush to bring them into this.

Bad blood could last a long time in the mountains.

At the same time Jill was making her way down toward Leon's place, Henry was driving to Knoxville to talk to Ivy's former boyfriend, Tim Cardwell. He wanted to ask him some more questions, this time without an audience.

Henry called Cardwell and made arrangements to meet him at *The Tomato Head*, a trendy vegetarian hangout on the old Market Square in the center of downtown Knoxville. It was not a convenient location for Henry, but he enjoyed the occasional opportunity to leave the damp mountain wilderness and visit a crowded, noisy, asphalt-coated urban landscape. It always reminded him why he loved his job.

Cardwell was sitting at a wrought iron table outside the café waiting for Henry. Seen here among city dwellers, Cardwell radiated the rude good health of a young man who enjoyed the outdoors. A tan set off his bright blue eyes and sun streaked brown hair.

Henry brought Cardwell up to date on his inability to get in touch with Ivy and then asked, "Remind me what you're studying at U.T.?"

"Bryophyta."

"Come again?" Henry said, smiling.

"Mosses and liverworts," he said. "I'm third year in the Ph.D. program."

"Is that the same as what Ivy's studying?"

"We're both in the Botany Department, but she's in Mycology. She studies Myxomycetes," Cardwell said, then remembered to translate, "She's first year, in slime molds. "

"Slime molds?" Henry asked. "No offense, but why would a young woman be interested in *slime*?"

"Oh, like anything, it can be intriguing once you really get into it," Tim said. "I don't share her fascination, but it works for her, clearly. She was obsessed. It used to be all she'd talk about, but then one day she suddenly stopped."

"How do you mean?"

"She changed," Tim said. "She used to tell me about what she was working on and sometimes even ask me for help. Then she stopped telling me what she was doing, where she was going. She got almost, like, secretive, as if anyone cared about her gnarly molds. Then she pretty much stopped coming around. It got to the point where we hardly ever saw each other."

"When was that?" Henry asked.

"A coupla months ago," he said with a sigh. "She's always spent a lot of time in the field, she's crazy about climbing the most humongous trees she can find, but the last I knew, she was spending nearly *all* her time out in the most remote areas of the park.

"At least that's where she *said* she was. I didn't really believe her anymore. We fought about it, a lot. Then, a few weeks ago, she broke up with me."

"Where do you think she's been spending her time?" Henry asked.

"With butterfly boy," Tim said, bitterly.

"Molyneaux?"

"Yeah, the chicks go for that French accent, I guess," Tim said, shaking his head in disbelief. "Gotta be something like that, because that guy is *way* old."

Henry was stung by the harsh view younger people tended to take of their elders, as if any years beyond one's own age were calculated in dog years. If Tim thought Molyneaux was *way* old, that meant Henry had to be *way, WAY* old. But he agreed that Molyneaux was too old for Ivy.

"Did the breakup make you mad?"

"Yeah," he said.

"How mad did it make you?" Henry asked.

"You mean like you think I might've done something to Ivy, to hurt her?" he said, incredulous.

"Did you?"

Tim shook his head, "I was into Ivy. I liked her a lot. But not enough to go all stalker on her." He looked at Henry, gesturing with both hands at the open pedestrian mall around where they were sitting. "Dude, look around."

When Henry raised his eyebrows for clarification, Tim added, "There's like 10,000 chicks going to school in this town."

"Are mosses and liverspots pretty good chick magnets?"

"Liver*worts*," Tim said. "Believe me, chicks go for moss way more than the pieces of lint butterfly guy is shopping around."

Henry considered pointing out that apparently Ivy didn't agree, but because he was *way WAY* old, he was too merciful to rub the kid's face in it.

CHAPTER 25

Leon lived in small, charming cabin he'd cobbled together from the remains of several old buildings on his family's property. The central part of the house was built of hand-hewn logs salvaged from a smoke house and an apple barn. Two rooms built of weathered oak boards from an old shed and corn crib jutted out on either side of the log cabin. The whole thing sat perched about eighteen inches off the ground on stacks of rocks hand-chiseled by his great grandfather.

The farmstead sat in a meadow at the back of his family's farm. His field shared a border with one of the most rugged areas of the national park.

It didn't take long for Jill to make it to Leon's place. But it was getting dark already down in the hollows and if she hadn't been there several times before, she'd never have been able to find it. There were no lights on, the weathered wood blended perfectly with the trees, and the cedar shake roof was nearly invisible under a thick layer of moss.

She stepped across the fence on a stile and walked through the pasture toward the gate nearest the house. The cabin was surrounded by elaborate, meticulously cared for herb and vegetable gardens. Jill didn't know that much about herbs, but she thought the gardens were beautiful, even though they were obviously not just ornamental.

At one end of the garden there was a row of beehives. At the other end were several rows of brightly colored zinnias to attract butterflies. And running along one edge of the herb garden was a half circle of large etched stone pillars. She'd have to ask Leon about the stones. She didn't remember seeing those before.

She climbed the steps to the front door and knocked on the thick wood. The curtains were drawn on the small windows on the front side of the house, and the place was quiet, so she couldn't be sure he was inside. His pickup truck was in the driveway, though, looking even more beat up than she remembered.

She sat on the steps and waited, enjoying the peace and the twilight view across the little meadow. Soon it was full dark.

"Hey Jill. Where's your car?"

Jill swiveled around to see Leon standing behind her in the open doorway of the cabin.

"Oh Leon, I'm so glad you're home," she said. "I need your help. Somebody's hurt."

She handed him the strange broken and bloody stick and told him about finding the injured woman. "I don't know what happened, but I don't think it was an accident."

Leon examined the stick and said, "This is an arrow for a crossbow. They call em *bolts*."

"It didn't feel right to go to the law. At least til we figure out what's goin on. So I come to you instead. Can you git her down?"

"Prob'ly," said Leon.

Jill turned to go back the way she came, saying, "She's up this way," but Leon laid a hand on her arm and said, "We need to take a little detour first so I can borry some climbin gear."

Twenty minutes later Jill stood guard as Leon moved around in the dark in a storage room at the dude farm Cloud Forest. He was stealing a ridiculous looking six-foot-tall slingshot, several coils of rope, and a duffle bag full of climbing paraphernalia used to teach wilderness skills seminars.

"Don't worry," he said, "It's only temporary. I'll bring it back when we're done and they'll never know it was gone."

"We're gettin close now," Jill said, as they walked along the logging road.

"I know this place," said Leon. "My grandma used to bring me here. It's got some kind of special climate on account of the ridges acting as wind breaks. Grandma said the Cherokee people consider it a holy place. Whatever *eejit* hurt somebody up here'll have a curse on em for life. It's like killin somebody in a church."

Jill was having trouble seeing in the darkness of the forest at night. She had to use a small flashlight. Leon didn't seem to need one.

"I think I'm sorta lost," Jill said.

"Don't worry, I can see her now."

"How?"

"Look up. You can see the reflective strips on her shoes."

Jill played her flashlight around til it illuminated the jacket she'd left tied to the little tree. Leon was uncanny.

Then, in the same way Ivy had used a crossbow, Leon used the *Big Shot*, the six-foot-tall sling shot, to throw a bean bag over a limb slightly higher than the one the woman sat on. It took most of his body weight to pull back on the flipper, but he was accurate and made the shot on the first try.

He tied a heavy rope to the nylon cord and reeled in the cord until his climbing rope was draped across the limb. Then he quickly rigged a harness and climbed up to where the woman sat.

He hung beside her and reached over to touch her neck. Although she was cold and non-responsive, he could tell she was still alive.

"Girl," he mumbled as he clipped her harness to his, "this gives a whole new meaning to bein *out* on a limb."

He pressed down on both her Blake's hitch and his and lowered them together, letting her own ropes bear her weight as long as possible. Then he clipped their harnesses together and made the last segment of the descent with both their weights borne by his rope.

When they reached the ground, Leon laid her flat on her back. "Need to borry yer flashlight," he said.

He knelt to lift the woman's eyelids, shining the light into each eye in turn. "Well, at least her pupils are equal and both reactive to light. That's good."

He looked her over with clinical efficiency and said, "Head wound's the problem."

Then he stood to retrieve and pack his climbing gear. He left the woman's ropes dangling up in the tree. He handed Jill the duffle bag and the Big Shot and hoisted the woman over one shoulder in a fireman's carry. He grunted at her weight.

Jill shot him a look and he said, "What?"

"The way you're carryin her, it's like she's a sack of potatoes."

"She don't care!" he said. "Hell she weighs as much I do! She's a hundred an fifty if she's an ounce! Built like a dang weight lifter."

"Should you be carryin her upside-down like that when she's got a head injury?"

"Trust me, okay? She's young, she's gonna be fine."

She didn't argue any further except to say, "Well, it ain't very romantic lookin."

Leon snorted and moved past her on the trail. Jill had to run to keep up with him. A few minutes later he mumbled, "I run up a mountain, do a hundred and fifty foot vertical ascent, and rescue some woman I don't even know. Then I *carry* her back down the dang mountain, by myself. That's pretty dang romantic if you ask me."

CHAPTER 26

Henry and Phoebe arranged to meet at the parking lot of a restaurant close to the Newport exit off I-40. Phoebe left most of her stuff in her Jeep and came toward Henry's SUV carrying a plastic grocery bag full of food.

"Phoebe, we're only goin to North Carolina. You'll be back home a few hours."

"Hey, this is regular work for you, but it's a vacation for me. I don't go on any road trips without Cheetos and Diet Coke."

"And Almond Joys," he added, looking at her supplies. "And Peppermint Patties."

"What's your point?"

"When I patrol the AT, sometimes I go out for five days at a time. All I take with me is half a dozen cans of pork n' beans!"

"Oh, you are *so tough*. I bet you don't even use a can opener. Do you chew a hole in the can or shoot the lid off?"

He pulled an absurdly thick Swiss Army knife out of his pocket and pried out one of the incomprehensible bits of curved metal and brandished it. "And I eat em cold."

"That's just … sad," she said, getting in the passenger seat and tearing open the wrapper on an Almond Joy.

It was a long drive to Cataloochee, so they had plenty of time to fill in some of the gaps created by the last thirty years.

"What're you doin back here?" Henry asked. "It's gotta be a big change."

"It *is* a big change," said Phoebe. "But it's a good one. I've missed everybody and I missed the mountains. And the whole reason I went into nursin in the first place was cause I wanted to take care of sick people. But every time I got promoted, I got farther and farther away from patients. Finally I just couldn't stand it anymore. I was spendin all day on a computer!

"So I came home and I'm real happy with what I'm doin now. I get to be on my own, out runnin the roads around White Oak. I get to see the countryside and all sorts of people and medical issues. There couldn't be a better job for me anywhere in the world."

Henry smiled at her.

"Do you like your job?" Phoebe asked.

"Oh sure. I get better at it all the time because we're always learnin more about animals and how to deal with them. When I first started, things were pretty crude, I was basically just a hog hunter, a pig exterminator, but we've learned a lot about wildlife management since those days. Now I get to spend more time workin with animals and helpin em. I especially like workin with the bears and elk. But still, this is no pettin zoo.

"What kinda stuff do you do with the bears?"

"Besides startin riots, you mean?" He sighed, "The bears are no problem. It's the tourists who are the problem. They create dangerous situations by feedin an animal just one time for fun, or so they can get a blurry photo to take home with em. But when they do that, they leave behind a large wild animal that's no longer afraid to have contact with human beings and who thinks of people as food dispensers, so I'll end up having to euthanize the bear because of what people have trained him to do. That's no fun.

"But mostly I'm doin the only thing I ever wanted to do. And gettin paid for it."

"Tell me what you've found out about the owner of the backpack."

"It's a young woman, a graduate student at U.T., and her name is Ivy Iverson. I talked to her professor, her ex-boyfriend, and a new male friend. Didn't find out much except lately she's gotten real interested in somethin in the woods. Nobody seems to know exactly what it is though.

"Of course, I'm still not sure she's actually missin. It looks like she is, but all I know for sure is she's not answerin her phone. She could be campin without a permit somewhere without cell phone service. Her cell phone could be lost or broken or have a dead battery. It's prob'ly nothin, but I wanna keep lookin."

"What do you think's goin on?" asked Phoebe.

"I've got a feelin the backpack we found was intentionally put there by somebody," Henry said. "It was in a strange place. It makes no sense that a backpacker would have left it in the middle of a field in Cades Cove. And Miss Iverson didn't go to the Cove much. It would be easy to carry it away from wherever she left it and drop it off where we'd be sure to find it."

"Why would somebody do that?" Phoebe asked, with a feeling of dread.

"Because they wanted to cover somethin up, like where that girl was when they took it from her."

"Why would you need to cover it up that way? Why not get rid of the pack where no one would ever find it?"

"Maybe whoever moved it, thought they had. Maybe they're not smart, or not as smart as they think they are. Or maybe they did somethin to her and were tryin to make it look like a bear got her."

"You think she might've been *killed*?"

"I don't know, but if she was, I don't think it was done by somebody who's from around here."

"Why?" asked Phoebe.

"Because we know a bear attack on a human in this park would look mighty suspicious. Our bears aren't predatory. Yet. And people from around here know how to cover their tracks better than whoever moved that pack."

The closer they got to Cataloochee, the more narrow, steep, and rough the roads got. Finally, when they crested the last rise, Henry stopped the Explorer and said, "There it is."

Phoebe looked down into the valley. The late afternoon sun was slanting in at a low angle, washing everything with a deep golden yellow light. The place didn't look real. It was an unspoiled paradise that made Phoebe think of Brigadoon or Shangri-La. Being from the Tennessee side of the mountains, she hadn't realized there were any mountaintop views left in the park where you couldn't catch at least a glimpse of vast clearcuts crammed with rental cabins. "Wow," she said.

"Yep," Henry agreed as he put the truck in drive and headed down into the valley.

"First, I need to check a bear trap," said Henry.

Phoebe cringed inwardly thinking he meant the horrible metal traps with jagged teeth, but was relieved to see it was an eight-foot length of three-foot diameter corrugated steel culvert pipe. It had an ingenious humane design. There were plenty of air holes big enough to provide good ventilation, but small enough to keep paws and teeth inside the trap. It was on wheels and had a built-in trailer hitch so it could be towed with or without an occupant.

"We set these out anywhere bears are causin a problem. We use em mostly in the spring near where the elk have their calves so we can catch any bears in the area and move em, to keep em from botherin the newborn elk calves."

He got out and looked at the trap, then said, "I'm going to have to rebait this one. Sorry."

"I don't mind waitin," said Phoebe.

"I wasn't apologizin for the delay, I was apologizin for the smell. I use sardines for bait."

"Oh."

"By the time I get this trap rigged again, I'll have the smell all over me." He grabbed a can of sardines out of the back seat and disappeared into the length of culvert on his hands and knees.

He was right. When he got back in the truck, he smelled

strongly of fish. The stink was enough to put Phoebe off the rest of her Cheetos.

Henry and Phoebe weren't the only people doing reconnaissance. Ivy's attacker was also on the prowl.

In the Hesler Biology Building at the University of Tennessee each graduate student was assigned a lab space for examining and storing specimens. In Ivy's area there was a pile of brown paper lunch bags used for collecting myxomycetes in the field and several rows of neatly labeled voucher boxes used for storing them in the lab. A dozen oversize Petri dishes were stacked near the window so the cultures could get some light.

Paraphernalia littered the countertop – tweezers, buck knife, 20X hand lens, glue, fanny pack, pens, filter paper. Ivy's attacker turned and took a quick look at the island in the center of the room. The students had communal access to a dissecting microscope for initial examinations and a compound microscope for closer work. In the corner was a tank of sterile water buffered to pH7.

He turned back to peruse the labels on the boxes in Ivy's area. Each stated the location where the specimen was collected, some with GPS coordinates, a description of the specimen, identified to species if possible, and what it was collected from.

Several larger boxes addressed to the U.S. National Fungal Herbarium in Maryland were worrisome. The boxes were empty, but that didn't mean that others with something in them hadn't been mailed to the repository already. Damn.

That could ruin everything. If she'd sent specimens to the

National Fungus Collections, he could only hope they'd be as good as lost among the millions of other boxes. The place was run by the federal government after all.

This meant he might need a bit more luck, but he didn't worry. He was used to getting it. The study of slime was often more a matter of luck than skill. It was well known that most people, even the experts, made many of their best finds immediately after falling down. The deep leaf litter in the Smokies was slippery and the hillsides were steep, so walking was hazardous.

But precarious mountainside walking conditions were not all bad news for anyone hunting Myxomycetes because one of the best ways to find them was in the leaf litter right after falling down a leafy slope. The researcher would sit up and *voilà*, the myxos would be right next to them.

You had to know where to look, of course. Some of the best places were under leaves or near logs in conditions that were just right – moist, but not wet.

But Ivy wasn't an experienced collector. Most of her specimens, especially the recent ones, were labeled as being found far above ground, up in the tops of trees. The altitudes were recorded, not just for the ground level, but also for the height in the tree canopy, 4,809' + 75', 3,987' + 134'.

He gathered up a stack of boxes and all the likely-looking notes, and took them with him.

"We're lookin for elk No. 32," Henry explained. "I don't know where he is, but he's likely to be hangin out with the rest of the herd. The elk generally come down outta the woods into these open fields at dusk. No. 32 got his trackin collar damaged during the rut season in a fight with another bull elk. I might as well change it out completely. He needs fresh batteries anyway."

Henry drove the park SUV slowly down the road that ran through the center of Cataloochee Valley. Elk were grazing on both sides of the road, each of them sporting large yellow ear tags with numbers on them and a clunky necklace with a plastic box on it. Henry called out the tag numbers he could see on his side, so Phoebe did the same for the ones she could read on her side.

"That necklace thing sure is ugly," said Phoebe. "And the earrings. Not an attractive look."

"Yeah, but it keeps em alive. The necklace is their GPS collar. Those things are $5,000 apiece. They record location data every few hours for two years. That way we can track the elk for their own safety and use the data for research purposes."

"Do you monitor where each of em goes?" Phoebe asked.

"Yeah and we even monitor whether the collar is moving or not. If it stays in one place for too long an alarm signal's sent to the monitoring station and we go check on em. Elk were extinct in this area until recently, hunters had killed every one of em. But we got some reintroduction stock sent here in 2001 to try to start over. A few of em are still tryin to get back home. If they wander too close to the Interstate, we go get em and bring em back to Cataloochee."

Phoebe laughed, thinking he was joking.

"I'm not kiddin," Henry said. "Number 7 got all the way across I-40, over two stone retaining walls, the median, everything, and when we tried to catch him he ran back across in the opposite direction. You should've seen him."

"Is he okay?"

"He's fine. Prob'ly plottin another breakout as we speak."

"Each of the collars broadcasts on a slightly different frequency, so we know which elk each signal is comin from. The University uses somethin similar on bears. Last winter one of the graduate students was sent to the park to check on a bear that was in hibernation.

"The kid hiked in to where the bear's territory was historically known to be. Then he turned on the trackin device that monitors the bears' collars and tuned it to the frequency of the bear he was lookin for.

"He got a *real strong* signal. When that happens, it's a big relief because it means you're close to the place you're lookin for. He walked around, tryin to spot a den, but he couldn't see it. He thrashed around in the woods for hours, gettin more and more frustrated and worn out, basically goin round and round in circles, but he never could find the bear.

"Finally he gave up and drove back to Knoxville. He called his professor and told him what'd happened. The professor asked the kid to take a look in his backpack at the extra collar he'd been carryin in case he'd needed to change out the one on the bear. He told him to see if the backup collar had somehow gotten switched *on*.

"It had. The student checked the central log book and discovered that the spare collar he'd been carryin broadcasted on a frequency close to that of the collar he'd been tryin to locate.

"So, he'd spent the better part of a day of crashin around in the wilderness, followin his own backpack."

Phoebe burst out laughing and Henry joined in.

"Taking care of critters is harder than people think," he said.

Taking care of people is even harder, he thought, but didn't say. He was thinking about the temperature at high altitudes of the park, the wind and the damp, and worrying that if the girl was out there somewhere she might die from exposure. Especially if she was hurt. But he didn't say anything because Phoebe had enough sadness in her life.

CHAPTER 27

It was twilight by the time Henry finally spotted the rascally elk No. 32. He needed to be able to catch the animal, so he loaded up a special cocktail of drugs into a dart. He was quick, cool, and efficient. Thank goodness there was no crowd to worry about this time.

"What're you usin?" Phoebe asked.

"Carfentanil, it's something like 10,000 times more potent than morphine." Henry carefully inserted the sharp end of a long needle into the *hole* in the sharp end of the needle on the dart. It looked like the two needles were trying to stab each other to death. Phoebe'd never seen anyone do that before. It made refueling a jet in mid-air look crude by comparison.

"Why are you doin that?" she asked.

"This drug can be lethal to humans if it's not used properly," Henry said. "I don't want any of it splashin onto a mucous membrane."

Phoebe took a step back.

The next few minutes was so similar to countless scenes in documentary films it didn't seem real until Henry asked her to hold the elk's head up while he worked on it. As she stood holding the big fellow, Phoebe touched his antlers and was surprised at how warm they were, and velvety. "His antlers are hot!" she said.

"Yeah, when they're growin out they're like that they have a good blood supply. Their rate of growth is a real biological phenomenon, one of the fastest growin things on earth. Later they harden and the velvet gets scraped off. They're cold then, and then finally, they shed them. Phoebe had a belated thought and quickly checked her hands in the dwindling light to make sure she'd wiped them clean before handling the elk. Thank goodness she had. She thought, embarrassed, *you might be a redneck if you petted a wild elk and left Cheeto stripes on its fur.*

Henry examined the elk, gave it an injection of antibiotics, and took some measurements. Then he changed out its collar. By then it was full dark. Really dark, like only a wilderness on a cloudy night can be. Phoebe hadn't moved, so she knew she had to be standing within a few feet of where Henry and the elk were, but she couldn't see either of them. She had no idea what was going on. Then she heard a strange grunt in the gloom.

Phoebe had grown up on a farm and knew better than to talk when a person was working closely with a skittish animal, but she couldn't help herself. "Henry, is that you makin that noise?" she whispered.

"No!" he sputtered, sounding exasperated.

A few minutes later he said in a warning tone, "I'm injectin the reversal drug now."

Phoebe barely understood what he'd said, but at his tone of voice she bolted, stumbling clumsily across the murky field, a flurry of guttural noises and harsh breathing exploding out of the darkness at her back.

When she was safely behind the hood of the Explorer, Phoebe turned toward the meadow and waited, virtually blind. It was several minutes filled with more grunting before a human-sized shadow stepped calmly up onto the road beside her.

"You okay?" Phoebe asked the indistinct shape. "Uh huh," Henry said, out of breath.

"What was all that scufflin and racket?" she asked.

"Can't let go of em too quick," he said. "You wanna make sure they're good and awake before you let em loose. I wouldn't want him be walkin around groggy this close to a river. He might fall in and drown."

Ah, like the angel who'd wrestled with Jacob at the Jabbok ford. But mercifully, in this battle neither participant had been lamed. The worst that happened was the elk got a brand new funny-looking necklace.

Phoebe began to realize that as a routine part of his job Henry had to wrestle bears, elk, and pretty much anything with fangs, tusks, claws, or horns. She mentally compared fighting large wild animals with fighting Wanda over a box of doughnuts.

Henry had a huge advantage though, Phoebe wasn't allowed to use a dart gun on her patients no matter how hard they were to handle. She made a mental note to mention this to Waneeta. A dart gun would be perfect for dealing with Wanda.

Henry was a professional critter wrangler, and had been one for thirty years. That was how he'd earned his living. She wasn't sure why, but somehow, his having physical courage at night, in total darkness, seemed even more impressive than being brave during the day. Phoebe often felt brave first thing in the morning, but in the dark she was a big chicken.

"How many wildlife rangers are there?" Phoebe asked.

"Five," said Henry, "but two are part-time."

"*Five?*"

Phoebe marveled that a handful of people were responsible for the wildlife in the Smokies, *all* the animals in the 800 square mile, 520,000 acre park. Five guys, two of them part-time, were supposed to oversee *all* the animals in the park.

"When do you sleep?"

"In the winter when the bears do," Henry said. "In the last four months I've put in five weeks worth of overtime."

It had never occurred to Phoebe that rangers would have to work day and night. This night shift work out in the sticks, handling wild animals, was something she'd never thought about before. She wondered if it was any less scary for Henry to do his job if he couldn't see what he was doing?

Later, in the wee hours of the morning, they sat together in the Explorer atop a ridge astride the North Carolina-Tennessee state line. Henry said, "Here, try this on," and offered her a confusing web of black elastic straps laced through the fingers of both hands.

"What is it?" Phoebe asked. "Some sort of thong thing? You can forget about it, mister." She was really disappointed in Henry. She'd thought he was different.

"It's not a thong! It goes on your head for goodness sake," he explained as he reached out to roughly position the straps. "You'll like it, Phoebe, I promise."

"I've heard that before," she mumbled, but allowed him to place the mysterious snarl of fabric over her hair and adjust it. It was part hairnet and part helmet. It seemed designed not to protect your head from injury, but only to hold the major bits of it in place in the event of a serious accident.

Then something like a jeweler's loupe dropped down to cover her right eye. "Oh my Lord!" she said. "It's night vision!"

She swiveled her head to scan the woods around where they were sitting. "This is amazing! I can see *better* than in daylight! How's that possible?"

Phoebe expected the Americans to have something better than the only other night vision optics she'd ever used – the Russian military surplus gear her father had borrowed years ago from a friend. All she and her father had ever used it for was to watch possums amble through the yard in the dark. The old Russian technology was built like a heavy oversized pair of binoculars. And the image it produced had been disappointingly green and fuzzy.

This was something else all together. It was wonderful.

"It's third generation optics," Henry said. "For only six thousand dollars, you can have one just like it."

"Six thousand dollars?" she repeated, fiddling with the monocle and the headbands to get the eyepiece just right. "Well, if you've got the money, this wouldn't be a bad way to spend it. I can distinguish every leaf and twig out there. My poor human eyeballs can't manage that under any light conditions."

She swiveled on the seat to face him and lifted the monocle up, "This is some pretty pervy stuff. Tell me, what's the freakiest thing you've ever done with it? And don't lie."

He laughed, then held up his right hand like he was swearing and said, "Aside from strictly regulation activities, I've only ever used it to hide from people who were comin toward me on a trail when I wasn't in a talkin mood."

"By *not in a talking mood*, you mean not wantin to be discovered hikin in the park at night in full camo with a silenced sniper rifle and night vision?"

He smiled and nodded, "Exactly. When I'm hog huntin, if anybody got a load of me all decked out like that, it'd give em the scare of their lives. They'd never believe I was a ranger and doin it for their own protection. It's better if people don't know we hunt hogs on the AT at night."

"If they knew you were out there terminating dangerous animals with a high-powered rifle, right outside their tents while they snored, with only a thin layer of mosquito netting or rip-stop polyester between them and … you."

"Yeah," he smiled.

"You're *The Night Stalker.*"

"I am not!" he said. "When I was young I used to love to hunt. And straight out of college I was lucky enough to get a job right here in the park as a full time hunter. But, I've had to kill so many wild hogs, now it's just work. There's not much sport in it. "

He sighed. "Somebody's gotta do it, though, they're ruinin the ecology of the park, but it's too big a job. There's too many of em. It's ruined huntin for me forever."

She made a face that expressed something she hoped looked like *poor baby* but she was faking it. She was upset by what he'd told her. She'd thought of him as a sort of wild animal groomer, but a lot of his job involved killing. It was like a veterinarian having to put so many people's pets to sleep.

"Hey, I wanna show you somethin else," Henry said, sort of excited.

Phoebe wanted to make a smart-alecky retort, but she was too tired.

"I'm gonna warn you, with the night vision you'll be seein all sorts of different things out there in front of you, things you've not been able to see before. Sometimes you can't interpret the picture right away. This'll be one of those kinda things. Follow me and do what I say, but no talkin. Be as quiet as you possibly can."

He led Phoebe down a game trail for a hundred yards and then pointed at a stump and indicated she should sit down on it. Then he pointed to something else. She didn't see what he was pointing at and shook her head. He put his hands on her shoulders to hold her in place and flipped the night vision loupe down over her eye. Then, sure enough, if he hadn't been restraining her, she would've lurched out of her seat.

A pair of glowing eyes was floating through the air a few yards in front of her. Henry held her still and in a few moments she realized there were several pairs of eyes. Just glowing eyes, and nothing else. The eyes were bobbing up and down in total silence. Phoebe stared and stared, but couldn't see what the eyes might be attached to.

She was freaking out. She looked up at Henry sending him a telepathic scream asking *what is that*?

He reached down and lifted the eyepiece out of the way. Then Phoebe couldn't see anything at all. The eyes disappeared. There wasn't any sound being made either. She had no idea what she'd been seeing.

Henry kept one hand on her shoulder and used the other to

move the night vision loupe up and down a couple more times and it was always the same. With it down, there were several pairs of eyes floating in the air and with it up, nothing.

The hairs on the back of her neck were standing on end. She looked up at Henry again and he whispered, "Night-hawks."

"Birds?" Phoebe asked.

"Yep," Henry whispered. "They're not really hawks, they're more like Whip-poor-wills."

Phoebe looked again, less afraid now. The eyes belonged to night birds which were popping up into the air and then fluttering slowly to the ground. They did it over and over. It was apparently a little flock of them, all jumping up into the air and then floating down.

"That is the creepiest thing I've ever seen in my life," she whispered.

After a couple more minutes, Henry tightened his hand on Phoebe's shoulder and said, "I've gotta work tomorrow. And I need to get some sleep between now and then." So they walked back to the Explorer.

"Your job's rough enough during the daytime, I don't understand why you work nights, too."

"Cause that's when the animals are active and the tourists aren't."

"Oh."

"That's the whole problem with animals in the Smokies. This park is stuck in a choke hold, ringed by fast food drive-thrus, outlet malls, and rental cabins. The poor critters are all caught in a trap that's slowly closing in on em. More and more people are coming closer and closer to em all the time, wavin food or cameras in their faces. I'm just trying to help keep em all as safe as possible."

"You got a hard job."

Henry nodded.

CHAPTER 28

"Open the tailgate, will ye?" Leon asked Jill. He bent over and, as gently as possible, he sat the unconscious woman down on the tailgate of his pickup, then carefully laid her on her back. "I need to borry that flashlight again," he said.

He stooped to take another look at the woman's eyes. "She's had a hard lick on the head," Leon said, "but she's already lived through the worst of it."

Jill looked at the woman with concern.

"Where to now?" Leon asked.

"Should we take her to the hospital down in Knoxville?" Jill asked.

"Ordinarily I'd say yes, but somebody is tryin to kill this girl. Maybe they think they already have. But if we take her to the hospital it'll get in the news and they'll know she's still alive. "

Jill looked at the unconscious girl with concern.

"The cops don't have any jurisdiction in the park," Leon said, "and the Park Service won't git anywhere investigatin somethin like this. Nobody around here will tell em anything.

"We've got a better chance of findin out what's goin on than they do. She'll be safer with us til we git things figured out."

"Well, I can keep her at my place," Jill said.

Leon drove them to Hamilton's, carried the girl in, and placed her on a day bed in Jill's studio.

"She'll be okay," he said.

"How can you tell?"

"Her breathin and color are good, better than they was when we found her, and her heart's strong." He lifted a corner of her jacket and said, "Her clothes are wet, but it hadn't rained. She's been up there for hours to collect that much moisture. Prob'ly overnight. So she's strong. All anybody can do at this point is just keep her warm and wait."

Jill deferred to Leon because she knew he'd had the special first aid training. She sent Leon out of the room while she undressed the woman, bathed her, examined her for injuries, and put her into a clean nightgown. She tucked her under a pile of warm covers, then called him back in to tell him what she'd found.

"She's got the head wound, some scratches on her hands, and two awful bruises on her body, one on the back and another on a thigh. The only other marks on her are chap marks from the harness straps around her legs and waist."

He nodded, then sat down in a chair next to the bed, saying, "I'll watch her."

"Who do you think she is?" Jill said.

"No idea," Leon replied. "Could be from anywhere."

"Clothes look American."

"Well, that narrows it down," Leon said.

"Do you reckon it was an accident?"

"No. You don't leave a person stranded with a head wound unless you mean business."

"Maybe she had someone with her who went for help and got lost," Jill said.

"I don't think that's what happened. Like you said, where's her stuff? And surely if anybody'd been with her, they'd've tied a rag on the tree or marked the place in some way. If you didn't leave some sort of sign in a place like that, you might not be able to find her again. It'd be hard enough to find her again, even if you did."

"Surely there's not very many people who can climb like that," Jill said. "So maybe she's in some sort of club. They might be able to tell us who she is."

"I better tell Phoebe about this," she said as she dialed the phone, but there was no answer. "What should we do now?"

"We better be careful who we talk to," said Leon. "Why don't you go on to sleep. I'll stay with her. I promise I'll come get you if anything changes."

Leon watched over the unconscious woman throughout the long night.

He sat beside her bed until it was almost morning. When he heard Jill moving around, he went to knock on the door to her bedroom and said softly through the door, "Jill, it's time for me to take off. She's still sleepin. There hadn't been no change."

Jill dressed and went to see for herself that the woman was sleeping peacefully, tried to call Phoebe again, but her phone was still going directly to voice mail. Then it was time to start making breakfast for the regulars. She baked biscuits, boiled grits, and fried up hash browns, bacon, and sausage patties. She made gravy with the grease left from frying the pork. Then she put on her game face and unlocked the door for the first customers of the morning.

When Doc came in to get his usual breakfast of grits and scrambled eggs, Jill leaned in close as she filled his coffee cup and said, "Before you go, there's somethin I'd like to ask you about."

"Sure," he said.

By the time Doc finished his meal most of the breakfast crowd had already cleared out. Jill had him follow her into the back. She closed the door between the store and her private area, saying, "There's somebody I'd like you to take a look at. He nodded and went into the studio with her.

"Yesterday I went lookin to see what that was flashing over in Greenbrier and I found a woman sittin way the heck up in a tree, passed out. Leon got her down and brought her here last night. Her color's been good and her breathin seems fine, but she hadn't woke up yet. She didn't have no identification on her."

Doc examined the mystery woman.

"You and Leon have done just fine," he said. "The only thing a hospital could've added to what y'all have already done would've been to run a drip of lactated Ringer's solution by IV, but that's not strictly necessary."

He adjusted the blankets and said, "Is there a reason you didn't take her to the hospital?"

"Somethin waddn't right," Jill said. She showed him the broken arrow and said, "The way she was when I found her, it didn't look like an accident. She didn't have a blessed thing with her except what she had on and the gear she was tied into. Not even some of the things she woulda needed to get up there where she was. Somebody had took them."

"And left her trapped up there," Doc said, "to die."

Jill nodded.

"Well, thanks to you and Leon, it doesn't look like they're gonna get their wish."

He shooed her with his hands and said "Go on and do whatever you need to be doing. I'll sit with her."

He settled himself comfortably in an old overstuffed armchair and propped his feet on the edge of the bed. "Go on!" he said, "Leave this to a professional for a change."

Jill gratefully left him sitting there and went to get the café ready for the lunch bunch.

Later, when the café had cleared out again, she came back to relieve him, bringing him a grilled cheese sandwich and some banana pudding. The girl was still unconscious. "Don't worry, she'll wake up when she's ready," Doc said. "In the meantime, after I polish this off, I'll go get Todd and we'll fetch your car back."

Only then did Jill remember she'd left it up on the mountain.

CHAPTER 29

As she drove to her morning calls Phoebe should've been tired from staying up so late the night before, but she felt surprisingly refreshed and peaceful. She found herself musing about the difference between saints and sinners. Often there wasn't much. In her experience everyone was a mixed bag, switching roles from minute to minute.

Phoebe's train of thought was brought on by the fact that she was on her way to Nerve's place again. A fine mist of rain was falling when she arrived, but it wasn't enough to bother with a raincoat. She parked and walked up a path toward the house. She was met halfway by a couple of skunks slowly waddling in the opposite direction, browsing. The cute duo made her smile. She stepped off the path and stood admiring their beautiful coats as they passed by. Skunks were among God's most striking critters, in more ways than one.

The skunks glanced at her briefly with nearsighted curiosity, not particularly concerned, and certainly not afraid. Of course they didn't need to be worried. The world didn't hold many dangers from a skunk's point of view. The only potential predators were large owls with hardly any sense of smell.

Phoebe pondered the fact that skunks were born with a bomb

strapped to their rear ends. Fortunately they weren't irritable. They were gentle creatures who always gave plenty of warning before deploying their weaponry. They'd raise their tail, prance around, and stamp their feet, trying every way in the world to warn you off. They didn't enjoy spraying. If you'd leave them alone, they'd leave you alone.

Unfortunately, your average human was not as merciful as your average skunk. Phoebe wondered why it was so hard for people to leave each other alone. She'd always felt sorry for people who went out of their way to kill spiders or wasps whether they were bothering anybody or not. Or people who enjoyed humiliating others or advocating extreme political views they knew were likely to be offensive to their audience. Or spammed masses of women with ads for unseemly products they knew none of them could use or want. Some people always had to be attacking something.

Most days Nerve was one of em.

Teresa, Nerve's oppressed daughter-in-law, let Phoebe in. "How's she doin?" Phoebe asked.

"Quiet," said Teresa. "Hasn't said a word all day."

The women raised their eyebrows at each other. They both knew better than to think that would last.

Phoebe went back to Nerve's room and sat down in the chair opposite Nerve's rocker without saying anything. She thought she'd just sit with her awhile and keep her company. That was another thing that was hard for some people to do, to sit with anyone in companionable silence. But Phoebe had learned that sitting quietly with a peaceful mind, just listening, whether the patient was talking or not, was deeply healing to both people.

To Phoebe's way of thinking, friendly listening without having any opinions about anything was the ultimate healing gesture. It wasn't easy to do, though. In fact, it was the hardest thing in the world. You had to shut yourself up first. Almost nobody could do that, or if they did, they went to sleep.

This one thing, *wait with me*, was all Christ had asked the disciples to do for Him the night before He died, but even the best men in the whole world had let Him down. Of course they'd all been men. The women around Him never let Him down. The women were always first in and last out, and seemed to have the only understanding of what was going on at all the crucial moments, but precious few bible scholars ever seemed to notice that.

Nerve's eyes suddenly opened. She looked at Phoebe and said, "There's evil a-stalkin."

Phoebe maintained eye contact with the old lady. Nerve's expression was clear and lucid. "Who's it stalkin?" she asked.

"The good people."

"Just the good people?"

Nerve laughed. "The devil don't need to waste no time foolin with the ones who's already workin for him."

Phoebe thought about that. It made perfect sense and explained a lot of life's injustices. "What kinda evil is it?" she asked.

"There's not but one kind," said Nerve.

Phoebe waited for her to explain. After a long silence, she continued.

"No matter what ye wanna call it, it all comes down to the same thing … because there's only one place it *can* come from."

"Where's that?" said Phoebe.

"Selfishness. Self-centeredness."

That wasn't what Phoebe'd expected to hear. She'd thought the older woman would say that evil came from the devil. "What about the devil?" she asked.

"There *iddn't* no devil," Nerve said. "Not really. At least not on the outside of us. He's *in* us. Just like the Lord Himself can't work 'cept through our hands, neither can the devil."

Nerve closed her eyes and seemed to drop off to sleep after making this last pronouncement so Phoebe had plenty of time to spend in contemplation of the insight. Gradually, she came to realize that this was probably the most profound truth she'd ever heard uttered by anyone on any topic.

It was possibly a Comprehensive Theory of Everything, the Holy Grail the physics people were always running around looking for. She wondered if she ought to put Nerve up for a Nobel Prize. But then she had to admit to herself that Nerve would be a long shot to win. Nobody ever won for an idea this important, this cosmically significant.

They gave Nobel Prizes for technical or political things. Things that made money for some corporation somewhere. Stuff the man on the street wasn't likely to be able to apply in his own daily life, as if that was a good thing, way better than something practical that everybody could use.

It was also problematic that the person who'd uttered this primal wisdom was certifiable, and in fact had been comprehensively certified and documented to be in the late stages of senile dementia, incapable of managing her own affairs. Nerve was a danger to herself and possibly even the surrounding woodlands should she attempt something as simple as boiling water or heating up a can of soup.

This did nothing whatsoever to diminish Nerve's achievement in Phoebe's eyes. What difference did it make if the wisest person in the world was confused about today's date by fifty years or so? The fact that Nerve didn't sweat the small stuff was probably what freed up her heart and mind for the really heavy lifting.

Phoebe remembered a movie where Russell Crowe won a Nobel Prize even though he had a bunch of imaginary friends. So maybe Nerve wouldn't get automatically disqualified purely on account of being insane. Maybe there was some fairness in this Nobel Prize after all.

A tolerance for oddballs and always looking for the best in people was what made Phoebe so good at her job. Of course it was a lot easier to take care of annoying people when they weren't part of your own family. That was another of life's great truths. Families were world experts at pushing each other's buttons. An outsider could handle cantankerous people without taking any of it personally or getting all wound up over it.

Phoebe was grateful to be in the presence of a soul as wise as Nerve and she didn't want to waste the opportunity. She decided to work on a song right then, hoping to draft on Nerve's genius. Maybe if she thought up some good lyrics she could convince Leon to set them to music. And maybe Leon could get Tim McGraw to sing her song.

Phoebe smiled to herself. Life could be such an adventure if you could just manage to stay optimistic.

CHAPTER 30

Phoebe left Nerve sleeping peacefully in her chair, waved goodbye to Teresa, and went back to her Jeep to look over her schedule and see what was next. There wasn't a single thing that she really needed to attend to. That was a peculiar sensation. That's when she realized her cell phone was dead. She plugged it into a charger.

Her curiosity about the backpack mystery was strong, so she decided to call Henry for an update.

"Hey Henry, it's Phoebe."

"Hey girl," he said sounding pleased to hear from her despite fierce growling noises in the background. Phoebe wondered if he was wrestling a wild animal while taking her call. She decided to talk fast and keep it simple. "Any news about the girl?"

"If you wanna play a detective," he said, "meet me at Twin Creeks in an hour." Then he shouted, "Quit that!" and hung up, or was disconnected. Phoebe wondered if maybe the critter had eaten his phone.

Now that the phone was charging, she saw she had several messages, but decided she'd rather meet Henry than listen to them. If she didn't hear them, she'd have what Waneeta called *plausible deniability.*

Many of the foray volunteers hung out at the Twin Creeks Science Center between events, because it was one of the few places in the park with couches, heating, air conditioning, and indoor plumbing. Phoebe arrived before Henry and decided to wait for him in the lounge area. From where she was sitting, she could hear a guy entertaining a group of forayers with an impromptu lecture on frogs and toads interspersed with bursts of mimicking the different species he was talking about.

He did a Copes Gray Tree Frog by trilling with his tongue, a Green Frog by making loud *gonk* swallowing noises like the ones you imagined everyone could hear when you were nervous and tried to swallow. The Upland Chorus Frog sounded to Phoebe like he was raking his thumb along the teeth of a plastic comb. Seconds after she had the thought, he pulled a comb out of his pocket to demonstrate an easy way for his listeners to produce the sound.

"Who *is* that guy?" she asked a man sitting nearby.

"Dr. Walter Van Landingham, he's a biology professor at Appalachian State."

"He's *amazing*," said Phoebe.

The man nodded and smiled his agreement.

When Henry showed up, Phoebe tore herself away from the frog man and whispered, "This place is cool."

Henry agreed.

"Why are we here?" she asked.

"I'm hopin some of these people will know about slime molds."

He walked toward the center of the room and asked in a voice loud enough to be heard by the group, "Is there anybody here who can tell me about Myxomycetes?"

"Oh sure," said a fellow standing nearby. "Fred, over there," he said pointing at red-haired man across the room. "Technically, he's just an amateur, but he's extremely knowledgeable about mycology."

Henry and Phoebe made their way over to Fred and introduced themselves. "We're trying to learn a little bit about slime molds," Henry said.

"So nice to meet another fan of Myxomycetes. It's a very exclusive club," he said, smiling. "Let's see, what can I tell you? How much do you know about them?"

"Nothing," said Henry.

Fred smiled. "You and everyone else. Okay, so here's the Cliff Notes version. Myxos love the Smokies. They grow best in temperate forests in the tree canopies of *Abies fraseri*, common name Fraser fir, and *Juniperus virginiana*, cedar trees. There are lots and lots of both of those kinds of trees here in this park."

"We're tryin to understand why a person might be especially interested in em," said Henry.

"Oh, slime molds can be extraordinarily beautiful!" Fred said. "Some of them are fantastically colorful. Others gleam like precious metals. You may or may not be able to appreciate them with the naked eye, but under magnification they're stunning. They're called 'the biological jewels of nature.'"

Ugh, Phoebe thought, *jewels made of slime.*

"Myxos are extremely mysterious organisms. They have characteristics of both fungi and animals."

Phoebe and Henry exchanged bemused looks.

"And they can be used to remediate ground pollution from metals like zinc, barium, cadmium, iron, manganese, and strontium.

"In addition to their anti-microbial properties, they're used in a non-toxic, non-immunogenic, biodegradable nanoconjugate drug delivery system. Polycefin is a cancer drug delivery system for directed delivery of morpholina antisense oligonucleotides."

Henry burst out laughing. "I have no idea what you just said."

"They're used for gene silencing therapy, for the transportation of antibodies and anti-tumor drugs to specific tumor cells, and they're being looked at as a medicine to slow Parkinson's disease."

Henry nodded as if he understood the explanation, but he was faking. Even Phoebe couldn't follow what Fred was saying.

"Oh and you can eat some of them. In places in Mexico there's a myxo they call *caca de luna*, that means *excrement of the moon*. They eat it scrambled like eggs with onions and peppers. I've read that it has a pleasant nutty taste."

"Sounds delicious," Phoebe said, lying.

Beauty under magnification, edible excrement, and slime powered robots seemed a rather poor motive for crime, so Henry asked. "Do any of these things have substantial commercial value right now?"

"Oh my, yes. Are you aware of the relationship between slime molds and antibiotics?" Fred asked.

Both Phoebe and Henry shook their heads. "Antibiotics are used to treat diseases caused by slime?" Henry guessed.

"It's the other way around. Slime molds are the *source* of certain antibiotics."

Henry and Phoebe were both surprised and exchanged a look.

"Because they grow in damp places, slime molds are prone to getting fungus and bacteria growing near them. And bacteria can be harmful to them, just as it is to us. Certain slime molds have developed the ability to manufacture antibiotics that will kill fungi and bacteria and humans have learned to make use of the antibiotics manufactured by slime molds to get rid of bacteria that causes problems in people. "

"So, it's possible that a slime mold could be valuable for a medicine?" Henry asked.

"Yes, the discovery of a new naturally-occurring antibiotic produced by a myxomycete could be immensely important to medicine and extraordinarily lucrative."

Henry and Phoebe exchanged another look.

"How lucrative?" asked Henry.

"Well, the entire DNA testing industry, billions of dollars a year, is built on the discovery of a bacteria that thrives at 158 degrees Fahrenheit. That's a hopelessly hostile environment for most life forms on earth. The bacteria was discovered in a hot spring in Yellowstone Park.

The DNA industry didn't exist until scientists who were attracted by the colorful stains you see around the edges of the hot springs found this bacteria. It takes a very special life form to thrive in that kind of heat."

"Holy moly," Henry said. "I had no idea."

"Since you're a ranger you might want to know that even though the unique bacteria used to develop DNA testing was found inside a national park, Yellowstone got no share of the multi-billion dollar windfall. The NPS got seriously angry about being cut out of the money, of course. As you're well aware, the parks are always cash-strapped. So the Park Service had the law changed. Now, whenever there's a discovery of a commercially valuable life form inside a park, the park where it's found gets half of the proceeds."

A man sitting nearby who'd been overhearing their conversation called out, "It's one of the marvels of nature how diverse the plant life becomes just a couple of inches outside the park boundaries!" The crowd of volunteers guffawed.

Henry thanked Fred and he and Phoebe headed for the door. They passed the frog guy again on their way out and Phoebe stopped, transfixed.

He was saying, "The Marine toads of Texas, Florida, and Costa Rica have a love affair with certain sounds. They're huge creatures and they have a low pitched mating call that is uncannily similar to the sound of truck engines gearing down. This means they have a fatal attraction to any road where there's a steep hill and truck traffic. They hop into the road looking for love and die by the thousands."

"Ouch," someone said, and Phoebe winced.

"We think of frogs as being noisy creatures. But the frogs themselves live in a quiet world," Van Landingham said. "They can't hear each other.

"Humans are unusual in that they have wide spectrum hearing, from 40 cycles per second to maybe 22,000 cycles per second. I'm older, so I can only hear up to about 16,000 cycles per second. But frogs' hearing is tuned to a narrow spectrum of sounds made only by their own species. They are totally deaf to the calls of frogs of another species.

"We hear a symphony of sounds coming from a pond at night, but each species of frog is sitting there in a silent world, thinking they're alone, waiting for something in their own pitch range that they're able to hear."

How sad, Phoebe thought. Frogs were just like people. It was so touching, and tragic. All of us were here on earth together, side-by-side and yet isolated by the limits of our perception. Lonely even in a crowd.

She would've stood there forever listening to the man, utterly enchanted, so Henry took hold of her arm and led her out of the building like a wayward child. Before she was pulled away, she turned to see if Van Landingham was wearing a wedding ring. He wasn't.

"That's the most amazing thing I've ever heard," she said as Henry propelled her toward the front door. "Can you believe that guy?"

"He's amazing," Henry agreed.

"The Frog Whisperer," Phoebe said, with awe in her voice. "Waneeta would *love* that guy!"

CHAPTER 31

Jill was cooking lunch. She boiled potatoes for potato salad and eggs for egg salad. She shredded cabbage and carrots for cole slaw. She replenished the urns of sweet and unsweetened tea and started the coffee.

The mystery woman was still resting peacefully in the back of the store with Doc watching over her. She'd not regained consciousness.

After a couple of hours, Doc came out for a break and sat on a stool at the counter drinking iced tea, waiting for Leon to arrive and spell him.

"I was wonderin if there's a special place where unconscious people can go visit each other that the rest of us are shut out of," Jill said. "A sort of spiritual chat room."

Doc nodded thoughtfully.

She stirred mustard into the potato salad, and said, "Whadda ye reckon is goin on in that other place?"

"I've often wondered about that," Doc said. "There are lots of people who live with one foot in this world and one in another. They're partially present in this material world and yet, at the same time, they experience a reality in another place, like Phoebe's dreams.

"I like to think they all keep each other company in that threshold place," he said. "The autistic, schizophrenic, and senile people. And the dead who watch over us, and maybe even the angels. I believe there's a community of souls who hover at the door between worlds."

Jill smiled at his description.

"I suspect they have the liveliest sorts of conversations with each other," Doc said. "We just can't hear it."

Finally, in the afternoon, during Leon's shift, Ivy woke up.

She was disoriented at first, and thrashed about in confusion, so Leon caught both her hands and held them gently in his.

"Hey there, girl," he said softly, "Don't be scared. Everythang's alright. You're safe now."

His voice calmed her. She stopped flailing and lay with her eyes open, trying to focus on him and then the room.

"Can't see," she mumbled hoarsely, "... all blurry."

"You got a hard lick on yer noggin. We found you sittin way up in a big old tree. We fetched ye down here to White Oak, but we didn't tell nobody what we done, so whoever did this to ye, they got no idea whur you're at. You're hid real good. Nobody can find ye here," Leon said. "Can you tell me what happened?"

"Shot," she croaked in a ragged, weak voice. "Somebody ... got my crossbow."

"Do you know who it was?"

"No."

"Can you think of anybody who might wanna hurt you?"

She shook her head slightly. He could tell the movement made her dizzy because she closed her eyes.

"Is there anybody you'd like me to call for you?" Leon asked.

She clutched his hand, and said in a husky whisper, "Jameson Knob … black light the cabinet … wait … glow after five seconds … get those. Please … don't tell any … ."

He felt her grip loosen. She'd lost consciousness again.

CHAPTER 32

Henry and Phoebe had parted ways so each of them could continue their work day. After Phoebe drove off, Henry decided to take another trip to Knoxville, this time to the Biology Department at the University of Tennessee, making sure to time his visit during a Myxo Madness event that Professor Whittington was leading so he wouldn't be around. Henry would normally have removed his flat hat as he entered a building, but with it on, he knew he represented a trusted and beloved American icon. He needed all the help he could get with his investigation, even if it was from a costume, so he left it on.

He perused the building directory, then followed arrows on the wall, reading the label on every door as he walked down a long hallway. Near the far end he found the Dean's office. A pretty young girl with bright blue hair was manning the reception desk. Henry smiled at her and tried to look lost.

"Whatcha lookin for?" she said with an answering smile.

"I'm not sure," Henry replied.

"Well, then you've come to the right place," she said. "Take a fella like you outta the woods and set em down in a place like this and they git all discombobulated, don't they? A compass won't do you a bit of good in here."

"True," said Henry.

"How can I help?"

Henry looked at her and decided a friendly blue-haired girl would appreciate the direct approach, so he said softly, "I'm tryin to get the dirt on Conrad Whittington, if there is any."

"Oh," she said, pursing her lips as she glanced over her shoulder. She swiveled her chair so her back was to her boss's door.

"Anything you're willin to tell me?" he said speaking quietly.

The girl whispered, "Is he in trouble?"

"He might be," Henry said, leaning in so he could whisper, too.

"Good. Cause he's a sleaze ball."

"Oh really?" Henry said, leaning even closer. "Do tell."

She thought for a moment, then said, "He likes people to think he's just a boring old fart, but he's mean as hell. A predator. And a bully."

Henry raised his eyebrows.

"The word is that Ph.D. candidates around him have a tendency to drop out without getting a degree, several of them after completing all the course work and turning in dissertations. Nobody seems to know why. Whatever's going on there, so far he's been able to cover his tracks.

"He's been divorced several times, prob'ly because he chases women students. His ex-wives hate him and are after him for unpaid alimony. Lotsa people call here complainin about delays in us depositing his salary checks. But that's some cock 'n bull story he's givin out," she whispered so softly he was nearly lip reading.

Anything else she'd been about to say was prevented by the entrance of a short, balding man who stepped out of the inner office and said, "Jolene, this is a place of business, not a night club."

Then he turned to Henry, who was still leaning close to the girl, and said in an unfriendly tone, "May I help you?"

It was obvious that Henry wouldn't be getting any useful information from the Dean, and the girl's sudden stiffening made him cautious, so he winked at her and said, "Not unless you can make this sweet thing go out with me."

Then before the Dean had time to throw him out, he left, waving a friendly goodbye to Jolene.

Henry wandered the halls until he found a door that said "Mycology Lab." Three young people walked by carrying trays of bark with oozing growths on them. There were two men and a woman. He followed them inside.

After they'd set their trays down, he asked, "Any of you folks have classes with Whittington?"

His authoritative looks and the way he left off the Professor's title made them curious.

"I do," said the guy who was wearing a baseball cap.

"I'm tryin to find out whatever you're willin to tell me about him."

None of the students said anything.

"I don't need to know your names," Henry said. "And what you tell me won't go any further. I know he isn't what he seems."

The three exchanged looks, then the woman spoke, "He's a creep," she said. "Always hitting on the women. If you say *no*, he acts like he was just kidding, but then you get a bad grade."

"He's notorious for using students as research assistants and then stealing their work," said the taller of the men. "Everybody knows he does it, but nothing's ever done to stop him. I mean, lots of the profs do that, it's sort of how things work at a university, but, he's the *worst*. And when he's confident he won't get caught, he's ruthless. Just ask some of the people he's used and then forced out of the doctoral program."

"Yeah, he acts sorta geeky, like he's absent-minded, but it's fake," said the young man in the baseball cap. "He knows exactly what he's doing. Students are afraid of him, but you don't dare challenge him."

"Can you show me Ivy Iverson's lab area?"

"Sure," said the young woman. "It's over here."

She showed Henry how to read the labels on the boxes and the four of them looked through Ivy's specimens and papers, but saw nothing that bore a recent date.

"I know she's been going out a lot lately and collecting," said the student with the baseball cap. "I don't understand why her specimens aren't here."

"Where else might she keep them?" Henry asked.

The young man shrugged.

"Let me rephrase that," said Henry. "If you were gonna hide somethin you were workin on, how would you do it?"

"You can hide a myxo in plain sight and nobody would think anything about it," the taller man said. "Unless they were an expert, and even then it's hard to tell exactly what you've got."

"Where else might she keep specimens?" Henry asked.

"Jameson Knob," the young woman said. "I think she may have been working out of the research station at there. Maybe she's keeping her recent stuff there."

Henry knew the place. It was a large tract of mountaintop land with a modern house on it donated to the Great Smoky Mountains National Park by a philanthropic family. The house had recently been remodeled to provide living quarters and lab space for use by visiting scientists. The place was not used much, especially in the winter, because it was hard to get to. It was on the North Carolina side of the mountain at the end of a tough drive.

Henry thanked the students and left the lab.

He'd gotten what he came for. Now he had enough information to formulate a picture. Professor Whittington was a bully, a womanizer, a thief, a liar, and heavily in debt. In other words, a Grade A sociopath and a highly motivated criminal. What he didn't know was what the connection was between the Professor and Ivy's disappearance, if any.

But perhaps a visit to Jameson Knob would fill in some of the blanks.

CHAPTER 33

Although neither of them realized it, while Henry was at the main campus off Cumberland Avenue, Phoebe was just across the river at the University of Tennessee Hospital, next door to the world famous Body Farm.

She'd decided to take a few more hours off work and have a chat with an old friend, Professor Charles Goldman, M.D.

Charlie, a radiologist, was usually to be found somewhere in the vast windowless basement of the hospital because that was where the radioactive materials and devices were kept. It was a rabbit warren where most of the rooms were maintained in an eternal twilight to make it easier to read the myriad kinds of ghostly images the radiology department worked with: MRIs, MRAs, CT and PET scans, ultrasonic and fluoroscopic images, bone scans, and the so-called plain films, which weren't actually on film anymore.

Phoebe didn't want to use a cell phone inside a hospital, so she called Charlie's pager from the public phone that hung on the wall in the main lobby. From where she stood she could see the double doors marking the entrance to the Radiology Department.

When his pager answered, she punched in the number she was calling from and hung up. She stood next to the phone and less than a minute later it rang. "Hey, Charlie, it's Phoebe. I'm in the lobby, but I think this is about as far as I can make it without gettin lost. Do you mind comin to get me?"

Charlie laughed and said, "Smart move, I'm in one of the new reading rooms we've made since we've gotten computerized. You'd never be able to find me. It's one of the great things about this job. So many places to hide!"

It took nearly ten minutes for Charlie to appear at the double doors. He was easy to recognize even though she hadn't seen him in a few years. He was slightly over six feet tall with curly, prematurely silver hair and dark blue eyes. His coloring and starched white lab coat were perfectly suited to the silvery world he worked in. It was radiological camo.

He intentionally cultivated a professorial look with a closely trimmed white beard, but he was so muscular he ended up looking like a cross between Sigmund Freud and a pro football player instead. Charlie's beeper went off before he had time to greet Phoebe. He looked down at it and said, "Do you mind coming with me?"

Phoebe was happy to go with him. She loved getting to see all the images and watch him help other doctors figure out what was going on with a patient.

"What's up?" he asked, as they walked into the netherworld.

"I need some information on an impossibly obscure topic," she said.

"Ever hear of Google?" he asked.

"You're more fun," she said. Charlie was a genius who read nearly everything and remembered most of it.

"And the topic is?"

"Slime."

"When the topic of slime comes up, you think of *me*?" he said. "I'm not sure I should be flattered."

"You're the smartest guy I know."

"Oh, well then. That makes it okay," he said, smiling.

Phoebe gave him a quick overview of the information she had on the missing student and why she wanted to understand more about Myxomycetes. "So what can you tell me?" she asked.

"Hmmm," he said, thinking, as he punched in the code to a lock. He held the door open and gestured for her to go in ahead of him. She didn't recognize the room. The last time she'd watched him work, he'd been reading images printed on actual film. Clearly, that was now passé. She scanned the room for images to get an indication about which particular reading room they were in, such as ER, ICU, or Neonatal, but there were no wall-mounted light boxes with X-rays anymore.

There were several desk areas partitioned off just enough to block the light, but not enough to make them into separate cubicles. Each one had a rolling office chair and two computer monitors rotated 90° from normal so the long axis was vertical. He pulled a chair over for her, then sat down and logged in to the computer.

She loved to sit beside him as he read. The images of the human body were, to her, the most beautiful art gallery in the world. Charlie started talking and it took her a moment to realize he was answering her question and not dictating his findings pertaining to the image on the computer screen. The radiology department computers were set up for voice recognition and the switch to turn it on was handheld, so in the dark, conversation could get confusing if she didn't pay close attention to whether he was speaking to her or the machine.

"… the most important thing is that for their own protection some of them can produce and emit chemicals that will kill bacteria in their immediate environment. We humans noticed this defensive trick of theirs and learned to harvest and then synthesize the chemicals they create so we can use them to kill bacteria in people."

Charlie was accustomed to talking to himself in the dark, so he continued to run on without needing any prompting.

"Because of this, there's a renewed interest in checking out what's growing in the woods. You can get a Ph.D. these days in the finding or testing of novel biological chemical compounds. It's called *bio-prospecting*.

"And of course we've got a doozy of a hunting preserve right here in the Smokies because the place is a temperate rainforest, or cloudforest, or fogforest, depending on which area of the park you're in. Although a tropical rainforest is the best for many kinds of biological growth, a temperate jungle happens to be better for myxomycetes."

Phoebe nodded. She'd known Charlie would be a font of information, but it was still amazing what the guy knew.

"And we've got extreme diversity of life forms here because our mountains run northeast and southwest. Species weren't eradicated by the Ice Age in this area like they were in the Alps and Himalayas where the mountains run east and west.

"In the Smokies plants and animals could advance and retreat as they needed to, so they were able to survive. They didn't get trapped by a glacier and obliterated against the side of a mountain range like they did in many parts of the world.

"Give me a second," he said, leaning forward and typing with two fingers. An image of a torso appeared on the screen and he concentrated on it, manipulating it so he could view it from different angles. Phoebe was awestruck by the exotic rotations, slices, and animations the new digital imaging software was capable of.

Charlie dictated his findings in a rapid monotone. He spoke with a strong local accent, like Phoebe did, and she was amused to see that sometimes there were errors in the text as it appeared on the screen if he pronounced a word in standard English. The software didn't recognize it and he'd have to go back and say it again with an accent.

Phoebe laughed and said, "Jethro." That was the nickname his classmates had given him in medical school.

He turned and smiled at her. "The system is programmed to identify the speaker from the login information," he explained, "and to transcribe what we're saying. It pulls the examples we've loaded to train it to understand our particular way of talking. It can interpret the distinctive speech patterns of each of the radiologists who work here. I have to remember to maintain a consistent accent for it to work properly. I can't straddle two worlds in here, even though I have to as soon as I leave the room."

"Well, Jethro," Phoebe said, "I'm awful glad you chose the hillbilly world for your speech recognition. You're strikin a blow for hicks everywhere."

"Thank you," he said, bowing his head to accept her praise.

She sighed and said, "Now here's the hard question. Whaddya think's goin on if you gotta girl in the Ph.D. program who loves to climb tall trees and study slime, and all of a sudden she goes missin?"

"Is there evidence of foul play?"

"Yes."

"Have you ruled out the significant other?"

"Let's say so for the sake of this discussion."

"Then I'd say the kid's found something valuable in the tree canopy and one of the experts she's in communication with knows what she found and wants it for themselves."

Phoebe was amazed at his immediate and specific suspicion, but knew better than to dispute him.

"This is not a field very many people can navigate," he said, "even to steal each other's work. It requires a great deal of academic know-how to test the specimens. And then it takes a biochemist who can synthesize commercial amounts of the chemical compound discovered in nature before you can sell it."

"What's the most valuable thing she could've found?" Phoebe asked. "I mean somethin valuable enough to make somebody want to kill her over it?"

Charlie thought about it, then said, "If I had to guess, I'd say she's discovered a naturally-occurring antibiotic, possibly one capable of crossing the blood-brain barrier."

"What's the blood-brain barrier?"

"It's a great mystery," he said, turning toward her in the dark. "The human body is extraordinarily complex. It's not just a container where things slosh around together. It's full of discrete zones that are separated from one another. Substances aren't free to move from one place to another because that would be dangerous. For example, stomach acid needs to stay in the stomach. And there are sequestered organ systems, like the brain and spinal cord.

"An antibiotic pill that works well on lots of things won't necessarily treat a brain infection. There are filters in the body that carefully strain whatever gets into the brain or the cerebrospinal fluid. Many antibiotics can't make it through this filtering system, so they're useless to treat brain infections.

"These chemically-sequestered areas of the body are fascinating. You discover how unusual they are when you get a physical injury, a traumatic intrusion that breaches the barrier between these separated areas, so the rest of the body encounters it for the first time.

"Our immune systems keep a molecular memory of every type of body molecule to prevent them from attacking anything they recognize as a part of you, but when a new type of molecule comes on the scene that they haven't run into before, like when you have a cold or flu, they attack it.

"If lymphocytes encounter body parts that they don't have in their inventory list of acceptable molecules, they will engineer an attack on it. Unfortunately, this means when you get a traumatic exposure of a sequestered body part, like falling and getting a stick jammed into your eye, the immune response can go wrong and produce unexpected collateral damage to the normal eye.

"Immunologically the body will not be able to reliably recognize as its own some of the chemical components of the interior of the eye or of the testicles and this can result in peculiar outcomes after injuries to these areas. The body's immune cells mistake eye or testicle components as foreign invaders and attack not only the injured part, but also the normal part.

"So a surgeon might have to remove an injured eye or testicle before the unwanted autoimmune response can begin, in order to save the uninjured side."

"Good grief," Phoebe said, "that's amazing and horrible. I never knew that."

"It's interesting, but it's not really what you asked me. I got off the subject. You asked about high value botanical discoveries.

"Right now, about the highest value discovery would be an antibiotic that could treat tuberculous meningitis. That's a tuberculosis that can infect the membranes that envelop the central nervous system.

"There's a fierce, antibiotic-resistant strain erupting in India that nothing can treat. We have no truly effective medicine for it. It's scary. Any new antibiotics that might help with that would be priceless.

"So, my money's on a fellow student, or professor, or a biochemist who wants to take credit for identifying a hot new antibiotic that works in a sequestered organ system. I'd bet on the kid's professor."

"Why are you so suspicious of him?"

"It takes one to know one," Charlie said.

"Criminals?" she asked.

"Professors."

CHAPTER 34

It was late in the afternoon by the time Waneeta was able to get in touch with Phoebe. She wanted to have an undisturbed conversation, so she sent Bruce far, far away, this time by fabricating a story about a disgruntled local family, upset about the denial of coverage for an expensive experimental treatment to save their momma.

Bruce was deeply afraid of the local people. He worked in a rural area and was employed to care for the people there, but he lived in West Knoxville in a gated urban enclave with other non-natives. He dashed to and from work as quickly as possible without stopping until well within the perceived safe zones of the city.

He intended to leave before any unpleasantness occurred, but was being slow about it, so Waneeta faked a call to herself and then breathlessly warned Bruce that the LeQuire brothers were on their way over. As soon as he heard that, he made a mumbled excuse and left for the day. His car hadn't cleared the parking lot before Waneeta was dialing Phoebe.

But before Waneeta could say anything, Phoebe blurted out, "Waneeta, honey, I've found your 4th husband. He's fun and smart and talented. He can make every frog noise you ever heard in your life. You're gonna *love* him."

Waneeta didn't need to think about it more than a few seconds before bursting into song:

Froggie went a courtin' and he did ride.
He took Miss Mousey on his knee.
Said Miss Mousey will you marry me?

Henry headed to Jameson Knob to see if any of Ivy's most recent specimens and notes might be there. He hoped to find something that would indicate what she was working on and maybe even where. He'd been to the Knob a couple of times and tried to enjoy the drive through the beautiful North Carolina countryside.

The road was paved part of the way, but as he neared the research station, it became gravel. And the higher he got, the curvier the road was. Although the Jameson Knob Facility was part of the national park, you had to go outside the park boundary and take a long roundabout route through privately owned land before ducking back into the park for the last bit of the drive.

Along the way he passed the typical Smoky Mountain jumble of trailers, log cabins, farm houses, middle class brick homes, mansions, chalets, and old abandoned home places that jutted out from the steep mountainsides. He remembered the road dead-ended at a clearing on a high ridge. *Knob* was the local term for such a place and they generally provided fabulous overlooks.

When he crested the ridge he saw the stone and glass house set in a meadow with a 270 degree view of hazy blue ridges as far as the eye could see. The open field had been mowed close like a yard and was bordered with a picturesque split rail fence.

The place was spectacularly situated and totally isolated.

There was only one car in the small gravel parking lot next to the house. It was a black Mercedes Geländewagen. The car, one of the world's most expensive four wheel drive vehicles, had a U.T. faculty parking pass dangling from the rear view mirror.

Henry took a slip of paper from his pocket, and used the numbers written there to enter the access code. The lock on the front door clicked open. He stepped inside and gently closed the door.

He found himself standing in a high-ceilinged living room designed in a style popular in the late '60s. The main feature was a large double-sided fireplace set three steps below the level of the main floor in what used to be called a *conversation pit*. The room was awash in orange as the last slanting rays of the setting sun streamed in through a wall of floor to ceiling windows.

Henry didn't see anyone or hear anything, but his gut told him Whittington was there, so he used a hunter's tactic. He sat down quietly on a chair next to the door for the few minutes it took the sun to set. He waited without moving until his patience was rewarded. Only after the house had fallen into darkness did someone begin to move about. An interior door opened and closed, drawers were opened, rifled, and slammed shut. It sounded like someone was looking for something.

Henry stood up, took a few careful steps, and looked toward the source of the sounds. Suddenly an eerie blue glow appeared at the end of a short hall off the living room.

He did his special silent catwalk toward the light until he could get a glimpse of what it was. He saw a large man staring at a glass-fronted cabinet that appeared to be some sort of high-tech storage unit. It was Professor Whittington. He was waving a purplish light source that Henry guessed was a black light. He appeared to be using it to examine the contents of the storage unit.

Henry had no idea why anyone would do this, but he could tell from the intensity of Whittington's concentration that something very significant was taking place. He decided to interrupt whatever it was. "Hey there Professor! How's it goin?" he called out in a loud and hearty voice.

Whittington whirled around, blurting out a startled, "Wha…?" and nearly dropped the UV light. He nervously switched it off, so the room was suddenly pitched into darkness.

Henry clicked on the flashlight he carried on his belt and pointed it at the Professor's face.

Whittington was blinded by the bright light shining in his eyes and didn't see the phosphorescent green glow that arose from the specimens on the top shelf of the cabinet. It was as if a cluster of lightning bugs were winking at Henry behind the Professor's back.

Henry had no idea what the odd green glow was, but it lasted only a few seconds and then died. He toggled the light switch for the room and stood smiling at the Professor who was blinking and looking guilty.

"Goodness, sir, you startled me," said the Professor. "But I know you, don't I? So sorry, but I've forgotten your name."

"Matthews," Henry said. "Henry Matthews at your service."

Henry held out his hand. The Professor set the black light carefully on the counter and shook hands with him. "Is that coffee I smell?" he asked with the gentle distracted air that Henry was beginning to recognize for what it was – a cover for malignant cunning.

"Someone must've left the pot on. Would you like a cup? I

believe I could use one myself."

The Professor held out an arm to indicate Henry should leave the room. Henry didn't have any hard evidence, so he decided to comply to prolong the man's illusion of concealment. But Henry was becoming more and more convinced that Whittington was involved in something he shouldn't be.

He watched the Professor, assessing him, and made small talk, following along as the man moved from room to room, tidying up. Finally, Whittington yawned and said it was time to go home.

"I'll follow you out," said Henry, and he mimicked the Professor's earlier gesture, holding out his arm to indicate that Whittington should leave the building first.

After Henry and the Professor left, in an alcove in the far corner of the lab, clothing hanging from a row of hooks on the wall and the pile of boots strewn haphazardly below them seemed to become animated. A bundle detached itself from the rest as Leon moved out into the room. He'd been waiting, standing still, so he'd been indistinguishable from the jumble of windbreakers, rain ponchos, and fleece jackets.

He walked quickly to the glass-fronted cabinet, took out the specimens that had briefly glowed green in delayed luminescence, and put them into an insulated lunch pouch slung across his shoulder. He spread out the remaining specimen containers to make it less obvious which ones had been taken. Then he left silently through a window and walked a half mile down the road to where he'd parked his truck, returning the same way he'd come.

CHAPTER 35

Whittington would have to wait until the following day to resume his search of the Jameson Knob lab. Henry's sudden appearance and questions had forced him to leave the building. And then the ranger had followed him on the long drive back to civilization, so he'd had to forgo any notion of turning around and sneaking back.

Once home, he didn't even try to sleep, but sat up mulling over everything he could remember Ivy telling him about her work, as well as everything she'd asked him. She'd left no clear indications in her notes about to how to differentiate the valuable specimens from the rest of them aside from some obscure remarks about delayed luminescence. And she'd never told him how she'd managed the preliminary tests to determine the efficacy of the substance secreted by the new species of slime mold she'd discovered.

It was maddening.

When he arrived back at Jameson Knob the next morning as early as he could without arousing suspicion, he immediately went into the lab area and picked up the black light. But as soon as he glanced into the cabinet, he could tell someone had been there during the night.

Several specimens had been moved, and worse, several others were missing. Whoever had taken them had tried to hide what they'd done by spreading out the remaining containers, but clearly a significant number of cultures were gone.

Professor Whittington was stunned. Who could possibly have known about the antibiotic discovery? Had the ranger done it? It was inconceivable that a person like Matthews would be able to determine which of the samples were valuable. But if not him, then who?

And how had they known which ones to take? Was it an informed decision? Whittington was apoplectic. What if the thief damaged the important cultures? The thought was unbearable.

There'd been no indication on the containers as to which ones were which, just code numbers. *He* wasn't even sure which ones contained the source of the antibiotic. He'd have to run tests to determine that.

Had someone simply guessed?

Being thwarted at this late date made him so furious he was unable to think. The situation was intolerable. Someone was attempting to interfere with him. But who would dare? And where had they taken the specimens?

He tried to calm himself well enough to make a thorough and systematic search of the lab specimen cabinet and the drawers in the lower half. The identity of the person or persons who had helped her test the cultures had to be in there somewhere. The myxomycete community was not large. He knew every name of consequence. Possibly she'd gone directly to a synthesizing biochemist. But, whoever it was, he'd find them.

He was almost certain she hadn't had the opportunity to speak to anyone or conceal anything from him recently. He'd even reviewed the phone calls made from her cell phone after taking it from her backpack.

This wasn't over. Not by a long shot. Someone was going to pay for this. He simply had to figure out who.

As soon as she got up and going she dialed Henry. "Henry, it's Phoebe."

"Hey girl."

"I found out somethin I think you should know," she said. "A doctor friend of mine thinks the girl might've found a valuable slime mold that her teacher wants to steal."

"I think he's right," said Henry.

"How come?" said Phoebe, surprised that he'd gone for Charlie's theory so quickly.

He told her what he'd learned and she told him the rest of what Charlie had said.

"Well," said Phoebe. "It's all startin to paint a picture, ain't it?"

"Yeah," Henry said. "And we can add the fact that when a discovery is made inside the park, half of the profits go to the National Park Service. So, if Whittington gets rid of the girl and lies about where the find was made, he doesn't have to share with her or with the NPS."

"Do you think he knows where the girl is?"

"Yep, I do."

"How can we get him to tell?"

"I'm gonna go ask him," said Henry.

"You be careful, Henry."

"I will," he said.

"No, I mean it, honey, be careful. This isn't an animal you're dealin with this time."

"Sure it is," he said, and hung up.

CHAPTER 36

Lunch was in full swing at Hamilton's. Jill was busy taking orders, carrying plates to and fro, and ringing up checks. Phoebe waved at her as she came into the café and went to sit with Doc. "I gotta good story for you today," she said. "A genuine mystery."

She told him about the discovery of the backpack, the apparently missing girl, and what she and Henry had learned so far.

Doc frowned, but didn't say anything.

"Henry agrees with Charlie and he thinks Ivy might've made her discovery inside the park, which means the park would be entitled to half of whatever money's made off it.

"Henry figures the Professor didn't wanna split the money with Ivy or the park. That would cut his share down to a fourth of what it could be if he claimed credit for the discovery and lied about where he found it. But he'd have to kill Ivy to get away with it."

Doc nodded slowly, taking it all in.

"Henry's been real worried about the girl. He's afraid she might be hurt or lost out there in the park somewhere."

"Come with me," Doc said, standing up, "I've got something to show you."

He led Phoebe into the back to Jill's studio and opened the door, saying, "We don't know her name."

Phoebe saw a young woman lying in bed with a bandage on her temple. "Oh my Lord! Is that her?" she asked, incredulous. It was the girl in her dream.

Doc nodded. "Jill tried to call you. She knew you were worried, so she went over to Greenbrier toward where you saw that flash and found her up in a tree, unconscious from a head injury. Leon fetched her down and brought her here."

"Has she told you what happened?"

"Some of it, but she's only been conscious briefly. She doesn't have any idea who shot her. Apparently they used a crossbow that's part of her climbing equipment. Left her hanging in a tree, thinking she was dead or soon would be."

"She's lucky to be alive," said Phoebe.

"She sure is," said Doc. "That's why Jill and Leon didn't tell anybody. They wanted to protect her til they figured out what was going on."

"Do you care if I tell Henry?" she asked.

"No, go ahead. This will all have to come out eventually. But be careful, especially til you know for sure who's behind all this and what's at stake."

Phoebe stepped out of the room and dialed Henry's cell phone. He didn't answer. She left a message saying Ivy was alive and at Hamilton's and asked him to call her as soon as he got her message. Then she returned to the makeshift hospital room.

Doc was sitting beside the sleeping girl. He leaned forward to check the IV drip he'd decided to run to keep her from getting dehydrated and to give her the calories she needed to get well.

He saw Phoebe's worried look and said, "She's gonna be fine. When she was conscious, she was able to speak and remember what happened, so there's no damage to her brain. She just needs to rest now. She was out there a long time before Jill found her."

They backed out of the room and closed the door. "Killin a kid so you can steal credit for savin lives," Phoebe murmured. "What a world we live in."

Doc snorted.

"And to think a valuable medicine was out there all this time, growing wild."

"Modern people have gotten confused about where medicine comes from," Doc said. "Drugs have only recently begun to be concocted in a lab. Until very recently, they were *all* harvested in nature.

"It's fascinating how things used to be done. We've lost the old ways, like The Doctrine of Signatures. People make fun of it because they don't understand it. I've been reading up on it. Leon's grandmaw was skilled at reading plants. For example, one of the most promising cancer drugs, Iscador, is an extract of mistletoe."

"I had no idea mistletoe was good for anything except Christmas decoration," Phoebe said.

"Mistletoe is a strange plant," Doc said. "It was sacred to the Druids. It grows opposite to the way other plants do. It never touches the ground. It can only grow on the branches of certain kinds of trees.

"It thrives suspended between heaven and earth. It happens that cancer patients need this same ability. That floating quality is what cancer cannot tolerate. Cancer is a dark thing, a heavy, earthbound thing.

"Iscador lifts the patient up so the cancer goes away. There's a company in Europe that cultivates mistletoe on apple trees to treat breast cancer and on oak trees to treat cancers in men. Sounds crazy, but it works."

"Is it expensive?"

"That's the other thing," said Doc. "Plant-based medicines are cheap. The people who make Iscador want everyone to be able to have it, so it's sold at a price anybody can afford. Pharmaceutical companies have gone crazy synthesizing exotic manmade medicines and then gouging sick people for profits, but Weleda, the place that produces Iscador, hasn't done that."

"It's a terrible thing when sick people can't afford medicine," said Phoebe. "There's no excuse for it."

Doc nodded, frowning, and said, "When I was a kid, I got real sick once. Sick enough to die. The doctor came every single day for over a month to check on me, even though my parents had nothing to pay him with. *Nothing*, not even food.

"Old Doc Greene not only bought my medicine and paid for it out of his own pocket, but he left a dollar under my pillow every day, so my family would be able to afford to eat.

"He didn't have much cash money himself. Nobody around White Oak had any cash to pay him with. And he knew better than to try to hand cash to my family. He was a good man and he didn't want to humiliate my parents, so he slipped that money under my pillow to get them to take it. I decided that if I got well, I'd try to be a doctor when I grew up. I wanted to be like Doc Greene."

Phoebe smiled at him and said, "And you are."

"Well, I don't know about that," said Doc, embarrassed.

In the afternoon Doc decided to make a visit to the Esso station.

"Gentlemen," he said, inclining his head toward Lester and Fate.

"Hey, Doc," Lester said. "Can I offer ye a drink? I've got some of Blake Hamilton's finest, cured in a charred oak cask for more'n a year. Prettiest amber color you ever did see."

The ultimate moonshine for connoisseurs was not white, but was cured in a charred oak cask, so it had a reddish brown color like commercially-made whiskey.

"I'd appreciate that, thank you," he said, then took a sip of the high proof liquor as soon as it arrived.

"I need to ask you gentlemen for a favor. "

Lester nodded, indicating it was alright for him to go ahead and ask.

Doc dropped into dialect because it was so much easier to communicate subtle matters via the local patois. The sing-song tones permitted a range of nuance that was not possible in standard English.

"There's a feller who's not from around here tryin to cause some problems for a lady visitin over at Jill's place."

Lester nodded.

"He's a professor from over at the university. Mid-fifties. A big feller."

"That orta make him easy to spot," said Fate.

"I'd consider it a kindness if you'd keep an eye out for him and be sure he doesn't get up to anything in White Oak and especially make sure he don't get anywhere near Hamilton's Store. Just for a day or two."

"That won't be no trouble at all," said Lester. "Happy to help out, Doc. You've always been a good friend."

Everybody loved Doc. It was widely known that he never turned away any patient for any reason. And these men knew that although it was required by law, he'd never gotten around to reporting any of the gunshot or stab wounds he'd treated over the years.

"The man's likely to be in a desperate state of mind, so he might be wantin to have his own way pretty bad," Doc warned.

"That'd be a turrible mistake for him to make," Lester said. "Don't give it another thought, Doc. We'll keep him outta mischief."

"Let me git ye a refill," said Fate, reaching for Doc's glass.

"No thanks," said Doc, "I need to git goin, but you're right, tell Blake that's the best moonshine I've ever tasted. Even better than his Daddy's. It's *mighty* smooth."

Fate winked.

In the late afternoon, the weather began to turn.

The first sign was when the normally playful breeze petered

out. There was an ominous stillness to the air that dampened the sounds that normally carried for miles, echoing off the valley walls so everybody in a hollow could hear what everybody else was doing. In the stagnant humidity, hair frizzed and moods fell flat.

Tall dark grey clouds moved in from the northwest. And warm air, moist from the Atlantic Ocean, butted up against the tallest obstacle it had run into so far, the Appalachian Mountains. It rose to go over the ridges in a phenomenon called orographic lift, but as it did, the warm air cooled and the moisture it carried as humidity began to condense.

Visibility grew increasingly poor as the fog thickened. When the air got high enough and cooled, it would begin to drop the moisture first as a fine mist, then gentle rain, building toward lashing torrents that would cause flash floods.

People who noticed the darkening sky and cloying atmosphere drifted toward home to get their outdoor chores done, bring the animals into shelter, and batten down the hatches.

A couple of hours later the wind was whipping up clouds of dust and flinging it about in a stinging fury. The weather prediction was that by nightfall it could easily reach hurricane force at the higher elevations of the park, with ferocious, forest toppling gusts lower down.

Phoebe stood next to Jill and looked out the window.

"You reckon it's gonna storm?" she asked.

"Yeah," Jill said. "And I think it's gonna be a bad one."

"When it gets like this, I always try to remind myself that, even though I can't see it right now, the sun is still shining just as bright as ever and the sky's the same pretty blue, right on the other side of the clouds."

Jill remained silent.

"Yeah, it don't always work to cheer me up either."

CHAPTER 37

The girl had been missing for three days now. If she was still alive, if she was lost, injured, or hiding somewhere in the park, Henry knew the odds for her survival went down precipitously with each additional day. And now there was a storm brewing.

If Ivy was at high elevation, she could well die from hypothermia tonight. Time had run out. He had to find her. But to do that he needed to have another chat with the Professor. And this time he had to get the truth out of him, one way or another.

It had been a very long day by the time he topped the ridge, drove past the split rail fence, and came into view of the house. He arrived at sunset as he had the day before. The place was awash in the ethereal golden glow of late afternoon autumn sun. What a beautiful place this was. It was a genuine paradise. But just like the original Paradise, this one had a pesky snake in it, too. Henry didn't like snakes, but he wasn't afraid of them. He steeled himself to have a down and dirty talk with this one.

He pulled into the gravel parking area next to the house. And just like yesterday, there was only a single car in the lot, Professor Whittington's absurd black Geländewagen. He punched in the access code, shoved the door open, and stepped into the living room. There sat the Professor, in the middle of one of long low couches that were positioned to take advantage of the splendid view.

Whittington sat with his knees wide apart, one arm flung out along the back of the couch. He glanced toward Henry, but didn't seem surprised to see him.

Henry didn't bother to disguise his mood. He took off his Smokey Bear hat and ran his hands through his hair while he gave the Professor an assessing look. He could understand how the man fooled people. He just didn't look like a crook. Or a killer.

Henry could hardly get it through his head what Whittington had done. He gave himself a mental warning to remember what kind of person he was dealing with. He knew that a sociopath could fool anybody, even the best forensic psychologists and the most hardened and street-wise law enforcement professionals.

He took a seat on the other couch and sat quietly, facing the Professor, waiting.

"Hello, Henry," Whittington said, breaking the silence.

Henry nodded. "I need to ask you some questions, Professor."

"About ferns?" Whittington said.

"No," said Henry, "This time I need you to tell me about myxomycetes."

"Ah," Whittington said, but then he fell silent again.

"What can you tell me about them?" Henry prompted.

"You came a long way for a boring lecture on an obscure topic."

"Humor me."

"Alright," Whittington said, taking a deep breath and organizing his thoughts like the pedant he was. "The species that people often see most in their yards is *Fuligo septica*. It's commonly known as *dog vomit slime* and that's exactly what it looks like and is often mistaken for. Its plasmodium is a mass of glistening vein-like material that creeps over or around leaves, wood, or anything else in its way.

"The public, if it thinks about myxos at all, generally pictures them in connection with low budget horror movies where blobs come to earth from outer space and we're overtaken by green Jello, that sort of thing.

"Actually, most species grow on the bark of trees or on the forest floor in tree litter. They are quite small and usually go undetected. They are not mushrooms. They're not even fungi but some of them do wind up on mushroomer's radar screens.

"Several types are nutritious and easily cultivated. They could be used to combat world hunger if people were actually interested in doing that sort of thing, but of course they aren't."

Henry sat motionless, like a hunter.

"Myxomycetes are extraordinarily beautiful, but hard to appreciate without a magnifying glass. Some of them require a compound microscope with a thousand power magnification and an oil immersion lens to see properly.

"They're not well understood by science. In fact, we can't even agree about what they are! They occupy an utterly unique position on the Tree of Life.

"They've been classified in the Kingdom *Plantae*, Kingdom *Fungi*, Kingdom *Anamalia*, and Kingdom *Protista*.

"They contradict typical ideas about growth in that their species diversity is *minimized* in a tropical rainforest. Insects, birds, mammals, and flowering plants have increased species richness in the tropics. But not so for Myxomycetes.

"They love temperate regions, and especially the mixed conifer-hardwood deciduous forests in the US, particularly the Great Smoky Mountains. They dislike the tropical jungles because they have too much rainfall and poor air circulation when the tree canopy is too closed. They prefer the deep leaf litter on the forest floors here in the Smokies.

"They exhibit something like *intelligence*. They've been proven to be able to find the shortest pathway through a maze. That's quite a bizarre talent in a plant.

At that point, Whittington stopped talking.

"Is that all?" Henry asked.

"Hardly, but it's an enormous topic."

"I think you might've left out some key points."

"Oh really?"

"Want me to tell you what I think you left out?" said Henry.

"Are *you* offering to lecture *me*, about biology?"

Henry nodded.

"How novel. Please, proceed."

"I understand that some kinds of Myxomycetes produce antibiotics."

"That's true," Whittington said.

"And some of the ones that produce antibiotics make special antibiotics that can be used to treat diseases of the eye or the brain."

The Professor pursed his lips as if considering this idea, then nodded, "That's also true."

"I've been told that the kind of antibiotic that can get to special places in the body is an extra-valuable critter."

"Yes, indeed," Whittington agreed. "They're quite rare, and usually require tedious chemical procedures to synthesize the compound of interest, but yes, it's possible."

"I think maybe Ivy Iverson found one of these real valuable kinds of slime," said Henry.

"Are you joking?"

"No, I think she found it when she was climbin a tree."

The Professor smiled at Henry, but said nothing.

"And I think she told you what she found."

Whittington shifted his gaze to stare out the window at the extravagant view. His eyes narrowed to slits under the strain of looking directly into the lowering sun.

"You were her teacher," Henry said. "She trusted you."

Henry sat patiently waiting for a response, but Whittington remained silent.

Henry's phone had chirped a couple times during their conversation as messages came in now that he was back in range of a tower. At this point, his phone rang, but he ignored it.

"Go ahead, take the call," said Whittington.

Henry opened his phone and listened as Phoebe talked excitedly, telling him she'd been trying to reach him and that Ivy had been found, was alive, and was being taken care of at Hamilton's Store.

"What happened?" Henry asked.

"She hasn't been able to say much yet, but apparently someone shot her with her own crossbow while she was climbin a tree," Phoebe said. "Jill and Leon and Doc are takin care of her. She's gonna be alright."

"Did she say who shot her?" Henry asked.

"No, she didn't get a good look at the attacker, but I'd say Professor Whittington's a safe bet."

"I'm visiting with him right now," said Henry.

"Then you be *real* careful, honey," Phoebe said. "*Real* careful."

"I'll do that. You too." Then he closed his phone and sat staring at Whittington.

After a long silence, Whittington took a deep breath and let it out. He said, "Do you know what the difference is between being an expert on ferns and the discoverer of a new antibiotic?"

"Everything?" suggested Henry.

"Exactly," the Professor sighed. "Thirty years of stupefyingly boring academic slogging eclipsed by a kid playing hooky. One of my own students, and not a very good one at that, poised to become a rock star in the world of science. Rich beyond dreams of avarice. Famous. And the source of a great boon to humanity. A Prometheus."

Henry's lip curled.

"Do you dare to judge *me*?"

"Yep," said Henry. He stared at Whittington then quoted, "I give you Scorn and defiance, slight regard, contempt … ."

"Shakespeare?" Whittington blurted, startled.

"Yeah, I went to college, too," Henry said. "But I didn't stay there. After graduation I went out and got a job. Whereas *you* … you just hung around the schoolhouse *forever*."

The professor stared at him, obviously shocked to be spoken to this way.

"Never could make it out in the real world, could you? It's because you're sort of mediocre, aren't you? A mediocre scientist, a mediocre teacher, a mediocre husband, and as it turns out, a mediocre thief, liar, and killer."

"An assessment coming from a man like you," sneered Whittington, "means *nothing*."

At the same instant he finished speaking, Whittington reached back to grasp the end of a hickory hiking staff that was propped against a console table behind the couch. He swung the six foot pole in a savage arc against the side of Henry's head.

The blow ripped a gash in Henry's scalp and stunned him. It also knocked him sideways. Whittington stood up with the wooden staff and gripped it with both hands like a baseball bat. He took a step toward Henry to deliver the *coup de grace*, but Henry had enormous experience dealing with large animals. His survival instincts were highly developed.

He launched himself at the Professor and took hold of the hiking staff. The Professor was a big man and he wouldn't release his grip on the staff. Henry swept one of his heavily booted feet against Whittington's ankle and knocked him off balance. He went down pulling Henry with him.

Henry landed on top. He could've crushed the heavy staff across Whittington's throat and been done with it, but he didn't want to kill the man. Henry didn't believe in killing animals for trying to protect themselves, so he'd give a human being at least an equal amount of forbearance.

The tricky part was that most animals would stop fighting once they'd made their point, or saw that you'd made yours, but he knew better than to expect any mercy or rationality from Whittington.

The Professor wasn't in nearly as good a shape as Henry, but he was crazed and fought like a wild man. Henry was able to stay on top because neither of them could roll over while holding the long staff sideways between them. So Henry concentrated on keeping his grip on the pole and keeping it at chest level between them. That way he was able to keep Whittington pinned, hoping to wear him down.

When the Professor realized Henry wasn't trying to kill him, he let go of the staff and gouged at Henry's eyes. Henry had to let go of the staff to protect himself.

It was hand to hand after that. Henry punched, but Whittington pulled hair and clawed. It was like fighting a huge, monstrously strong woman. Henry expected to be bitten at any moment, but of course he was used to that, too.

In their struggle, Whittington rolled atop Henry's beautiful straw Stetson and crushed it. It was an expensive hat and its senseless destruction made Henry really angry.

The next casualty was an overturned side table with a heavy lamp on it. The lamp toppled and hit Henry in the back of the head, making an awful crack. He momentarily lost his grip on the Professor. The Professor shoved him hard and Henry rolled down the steps into the conversation pit, hitting his head against the corner of the stone hearth. The blow knocked him unconscious.

The Professor, exhausted, lay where he was until he was able to catch his breath. Even then, he had to use the arm of the couch to pull himself upright. Once he was standing, he gingerly made his way down the three steps to the fireplace. He gave Henry a savage kick in the ribs and watched the blood pool beneath the ranger's head.

Whittington dabbed at his face with his handkerchief and considered what to do next. He bent to retrieve Henry's phone. He looked at the most recent incoming calls and saw the local numbers. He listened to the messages from Phoebe about Ivy, then pocketed the phone.

He'd seen that ramshackle Hamilton place. It was a decrepit diner for the enclave of *Beverly Hillbillies* who lived north of the park. He'd be able to use the Mercedes GPS to find it.

He went outside and opened the drivers door of Henry's SUV. He removed the keys and pocketed them. Then he used the large flashlight laying in the console to bash the radio to pieces. He went around and jerked the back hatch open. He rummaged through the gear, taking bolt cutters and the case containing the hunting rifle and ammunition. He tossed the gun case into the passenger seat of his Mercedes.

He took the bolt cutters around to the side of the house where the utility lines ran in. He used them to cut the phone lines and smash the box to smithereens. Then he headed for White Oak with the intention of concluding his collaboration with Ivy Iverson.

As it turned out, it was lucky for him that she'd survived. Now he'd have a chance to fill in those frustrating gaps in his knowledge. Then he'd kill her and anybody else she might've talked to. From this point on, he would gleefully kill anyone who got in his way. He was sick to death of sparring with these hicks.

CHAPTER 38

Phoebe stood on the front porch of Hamilton's. A million shades of grey were roiling overhead. The sky looked like a film clip on *The Weather Channel*. Clouds of different shapes and sizes were churning and racing toward the mountains where they were clustering, colliding, and drastically changing the light from one moment to the next.

The wind was gusting, but not in any consistent direction, wringing tree branches in chaotic circles, like pompom girls trying to learn a new routine. The air was filled with dust and bits of leaves.

Phoebe could smell the rain coming. It was the sharp smell of earth and plants being power-washed a mile or more away. She loved storms. In anticipation of this one, she sat in the old naugahyde recliner and waited for it.

She could hear the sound of rain moving through the woods. It pattered against the leaves, getting closer and closer until she could feel a fine mist on her face, then suddenly it was raining so hard she could see the huge drops fall, hit the road, and bounce back up like they were made of rubber.

She looked toward the mountains but she could barely make them out. The haze, or *miasma* as the old people called it, was opaque.

Then the hail came. At first it was sleet-like raindrops that made a pecking sound, but a couple of minutes later she could see white bits of ice falling. It didn't look large enough to dent anything, but it was big enough to make a racket.

When the wind began to shriek and howl, she got up and moved to stand with her back against the wall of the store. The gusts of wind were propelling the rain in sheets that burst and subsided like waves. Thunder boomed and echoed off the mountainsides and the cracks of lightning were interspersed with the cracks of trees breaking.

When the wind got to full speed branches would be sent flying, then whole trees. Even now it was bad enough that Phoebe half expected Dorothy's house to land in the middle of the road. Time to go inside.

This kind of a storm delivered a one-two punch. First the steep slopes would get saturated with rain, then the wind would roar through knocking the trees over. Roots in shallow wet soil simply didn't have enough purchase to withstand sixty to ninety mile an hour winds.

It was worse at the higher elevations.

As Henry returned to consciousness, all he was aware of was agonizing head pain. He was lying in the floor. He remembered he'd been talking to Professor Whittington, but he was a little foggy about the rest. He struggled to a sitting position and looked around the room.

It was dark outside and no house lights were on. Then Henry

remembered the fight. He marveled that the man had been mean enough to beat him in a fight and stupid enough to leave him alive. When he could stand, he hobbled slowly around the living room, then made his way to the lab area, and checked the rest of the building.

It wasn't a big place. Soon it was obvious that Whittington was nowhere to be found. Henry thought to look into the driveway and saw the Geländewagen was gone and the back of his Explorer was standing open.

That was not good. He reached for his phone. It was gone, too. That was even worse. He picked up one of the house phones and it was dead. Of course it was.

He checked his watch. He'd been out for over an hour. He limped out to his SUV. The driver's door was ajar, the key was missing, and the radio was a mangled mess. He looked into the rear cargo area. The case containing the rifle and ammunition was missing. That was extremely bad news.

But the case with the tranquilizer gun was still there. He opened it and removed the rifle. He clumsily filled three darts, put them into a protective plastic box which he tucked inside his shirt, then slung the rifle diagonally across his back.

The night vision headset was still there, too. He picked it up. Again the Professor demonstrated that he wasn't as smart as he thought he was. Some people never learn. He shouldn't have left that. Without night vision, Henry would never have been able to attempt what he was going to do next. Whittington had a habit of causing people big problems and walking away without any repercussions to himself, but this time he'd messed with the wrong guy.

Henry walked down a rutted gravel path toward an old barn, went in and looked around with the aid of his bionic eye. He ripped away a dusty canvas tarpaulin, revealing a red dirt bike. The rangers used it for their jaunts to check on the webcam and radio repeater tower. The key was in the ignition.

He straddled the bike and kick-started it. The engine fired right up. He backed the motorcycle out of the barn and pointed it toward the woods. He prayed the kids in the Student Conservation Association who'd lived in the house during the summer had cleared the blowdowns on the nearby trail like they were supposed to. If they hadn't he'd never make it.

Henry had been a backcountry ranger for more than half his life, otherwise he would never have tried to travel through the wilderness in a long cross country shortcut, certainly not at night, with bad weather on the way. But he knew the park very well. He knew the hiking trails, the ones on and off the books, and he knew the ancient game trails. He could navigate the area better than any man alive.

He had to make it. If he failed, people were going to die. With the aid of electronically enhanced sight, he headed for a place at the edge of the woods that was intentionally allowed to grow up with tall grass for the purpose of hiding the trailhead.

If anyone had been watching the speed at which Henry entered the tall grass, they would've thought they were hallucinating. Then, a split second after he whizzed into the trees, he disappeared from view.

Phoebe sat with Jill in the cozy sewing studio while Doc read and kept an eye on Ivy. After a particularly violent crack of thunder that made the women flinch, Doc quoted, *We are troubled on every*

side, yet not distressed; we are perplexed, but not in despair; Persecuted, but not forsaken; cast down, but not destroyed. ….

Phoebe smiled and hoped he was right.

To anyone else it would be the least of their worries, but what nagged at Henry during his wild ride was knowing that the Park Service would fire him for sure when they found out what he'd done. Riding a motorcycle on a hiking trail was strictly forbidden.

Henry didn't want to get fired from the only job he'd ever had. He loved his job. But he couldn't let the Professor hurt anybody else. The man had done more than enough damage already.

As soon as Henry passed through a few yards of brush, he was on an old dirt road. The weather was terrible, but it wasn't raining here yet and the worst of the wind was blocked by the adjoining ridges and the dense forest. Even when the rain came, it would take a while for it to soak through the canopy and the understory to reach the forest floor.

He made good time along the road, but had to slow down when it petered out and became a hiking trail. Nobody but Henry would have been able to find their way in the dark. Luckily he had a lot of experience navigating the trails at night with mechanically enhanced vision, although he was certainly not accustomed to moving at this speed. It might've been fun if he hadn't been so scared for the people at Hamilton's.

Leon sat in the living room of his snug cabin in front of a cheerful fire, playing banjo. A lot of people would've paid big money to hear the performance he was putting on, but these days he'd only play during a storm when he knew no one would be able to hear him.

He was halfway through a rousing version of *Rollin in My Sweet Baby's Arms* when a feeling came over him that caused him to stop playing and set the banjo aside. He quieted himself inside and sat listening for a few moments. Then he leapt up from the couch and ran out into the tempest without bothering to get a jacket.

He drove as far as he could, then got out of his truck and raced up the mountainside on foot. His feet seemed to barely touch the ground. There was no time to spare. As he ran, trees were splintering, nearly exploding from the force of the winds. Exhausted, he dropped to his knees where he was, in the middle of the tempest, and prayed out loud, "Jesus Christ, Lord of the Elements, please help us." But the ferocity of the storm tore at his words and carried them away.

Henry slowed after passing a huge poplar with a scar from a lightning strike that spiraled the length of the tree, wrapping around the trunk like a vine. He knew the tree was near the turnoff to a manway that connected the hiking trail he was on to an old game trail. The track was called a manway because it was something less than a trail, but not impenetrable.

He jounced along through tall grass, low shrubs, and spindly young trees. The occasional briars were tearing at his uniform and not doing his hide any favors either. The manway eventually dead-ended into the game trail and he came to a abrupt stop.

He awkwardly walked the motorcycle around to make a ninety degree right turn onto what was basically a single rut, worn deep by thousands of sharp hoofs. He had to be very careful from here on out. His speed dropped considerably. The game trail had been used by all manner of critters before men ever came to these mountains. It was a path between a water supply and a salt lick. The first settlers had benefited from the animals' wisdom and used it for the same purpose.

This last bit of the ride was the toughest, and Henry was genuinely worried he'd miss the final turn. In the brief snatches of sky he was able to glimpse, he noticed the clouds were reflecting no artificial glow. That meant the storm had knocked out the power in White Oak.

That made it *much* harder to find the turnoff to the store. Henry tried to take comfort in the fact that a blackout would make it harder for the Professor to find his way too. Suddenly Henry saw a flash out of the corner of his eye. It nearly startled the life out of him. He thought for a moment he'd seen somebody standing at the edge of the trail, pointing. Then he stopped and looked back over his shoulder.

Leon stepped out of the trees and onto the narrow rut.

Henry turned the motorcycle around and backtracked to where Leon was standing, soaked to the skin and out of breath. It was the entrance to a narrow path that would take him down to the road near Hamilton's. Henry smiled to himself, not sure of Leon was real or if he was letting his imagination get away with him. But he had a head injury after all and could be forgiven for seeing things.

Leon hopped on behind Henry and five minutes later, Henry

turned off the engine and dropped the motorcycle on the trail, for fear of the noise giving him away. He explained his fears to Leon and they ran to the edge of the woods and stopped just before they might be seen. They might need stealth to make it the rest of the way to the store.

The two men presented a terrifying appearance. Henry's head and face were covered in blood from the gashes caused by the hiking staff and the stone hearth. His clothes were ripped and he was bleeding from his forehead to his ankles from dozens of superficial scratches and scrapes caused by branches and briars during his ride through the woods. Leon's clothes and hair were plastered to him and he was covered with mud and bits of leaves. In short, they looked like hell.

They felt like it too.

CHAPTER 39

The Hamilton's Store building was so old, the inner structure was made of massive chestnut logs. A couple of generations after the original trading post was built, after the park was established and life got a little easier, the logs were covered on the outside with clapboards to make the place look more refined. But the building had survived over a hundred years of storms, so everyone taking shelter inside the store was as safe as they could be.

Phoebe watched as Jill worked by lantern light, piecing a long coat from swatches of cashmere.

"This fabric is really nice," said Phoebe. "It looks brand new. I can't believe people sent sweaters like this to Goodwill."

"They didn't. Somebody left a box of em on the front porch a coupla days ago."

Phoebe looked up at Jill, smiling. "Gotta be one of the three Robin Hoodlums. Those rascals do all sorts of good deeds, but they won't do it unless they can figure a way of doin somethin illegal at the same time."

"Wonder who they stole the sweaters from?"

"No tellin," said Phoebe.

"Well, the rest of the rich people's sweaters are safe tonight. No one's goin anywhere in this storm."

The women laughed, not realizing how wrong they were.

Phoebe joked to Jill that the effect of the storm on White Oak was like a game of musical chairs. Wherever you were when the trees starting falling, it was best to sit down and wait.

The bad weather would isolate White Oak from any influences from the outside, either to help or to harm. But it would also prevent anyone who was in White Oak from being able to escape. Phoebe shuddered at the thought. She remembered Nerve's prediction and hoped if any evil was headed their way it would be held at bay by the storm and not trapped amongst them.

Professor Whittington didn't know how to handle himself in the mountains. For all his outdoor experience studying plants, he was still a city dweller. And, like most of the people who lived among gently rolling hills and flat lands, he had no clue what went on in the mountains during a storm.

He was headed for Hamilton's Store driving his hideously expensive four wheel drive vehicle like a madman. He winced as it jounced to the full limit of its shocks and bottomed out repeatedly on the rutted roads. Although the car had been made for off-road travel, Whittington had no experience driving it in such conditions. The machine had never been subjected to indignities such as driving on a road strewn with tree limbs.

The wind was tossing tree branches across the road horizontally, like trash. They gouged and scraped the car's glossy paint. But to

Whittington, it no longer mattered. Good riddance, he thought. The behemoth got terrible mileage. It was going to be repossessed as soon as the finance company could find it. He was getting desperately low on gas, but hadn't seen a gas station in nearly an hour.

But then his luck changed and he saw the sign. He didn't realize Esso was still in business, but he wasn't in any position to be brand sensitive so he pulled in and stopped next to the pumps.

He got out to put gas in his car and that's when he saw the station was closed. He should've realized it because the lights were off. He sighed and got back in his car. He hated these people.

Lester fired up his chainsaw and set it against the side of a tree trunk. He'd selected this tree because of its size, too big for one man to move, and for its strategic location in the middle of a blind curve on a steep hill. Only a fool or a crazy person would round a curve on a hill, driving fast on a night like this, but, from what he'd heard, that Professor fellow was one or the other, maybe both. So this was just the place to teach him a lesson.

The chainsaw roared, the tree cracked and popped, then fell across the road. Its trunk and wide limbs spanned both lanes and made a roadblock twelve feet high. Lester would love to wait and shoot the *eejit* if he came this way, but he knew that wasn't what Doc wanted.

Fate was felling a tree a couple of miles down the road on the other side of Hamilton's. They'd decided this was the easiest way to prevent unwanted visitors without having to stand guard all night. The weather was terrible, so this tactic wouldn't inconvenience the locals much because they'd stay at home, expecting trees to be down.

In a few minutes he and Fate could go to their own houses and get comfortable knowing the store would be well protected tonight.

The Professor drove for as long as he could, which was for only a couple more minutes. Lester had anticipated events perfectly. Whittington encountered the tree at 45 miles an hour before Lester had even packed his gear to leave. There was more than enough impact to deploy the car's airbag and knock the heck out of the Professor. Lester laughed. He'd gotten in a good punch by proxy.

Whittington was shaken by the collision, but determined. The impact had killed the motor, so he tried to restart the engine. The powerful beast cranked half-heartedly, but wouldn't start, so he got out. The wind-driven rain was ferocious. It peppered him like buckshot, stinging his exposed face and hands as he walked around his car, trying to assess the situation.

His discombobulation and frustration transmuted into a rage so powerful it broke something in him. He actually felt something snap. Whatever vestiges of humanity had been left in the man were there no longer. There was no longer any sense of proportion and no compassion.

He didn't think the store was very far, so he decided to continue the rest of the way on foot. First though he'd have to find a way around the fallen tree. He'd walked only a few yards away from the wreck when he heard a gunshot. He looked down at himself, startled, expecting to see blood erupt from his chest, but there wasn't any. Then he smelled gas, but before he could connect the dots the Mercedes exploded in a huge fireball.

The explosion picked Whittington up and hurled him into

the branches of the felled tree. He hung draped across a limb, bent double, gasping for air. It knocked the breath out of him. He had to concentrate in order to resume normal breathing.

He tried to climb down, but managed only to fall and land on his feet for just long enough to twist an ankle, then he hit on his rear end, driving the sharp end of a broken stick at least two inches into the meat of his gluteus maximus.

Lester lowered his rifle and watched the Professor's escalating misfortune with great amusement. This good guy stuff was more fun than he'd realized. He could torment a jerk to his heart's content and no one would fault him for it. In fact, they'd *thank* him!

Whittington rolled onto his side, reached behind himself, and jerked the stick out of his butt, howling like a banshee at the pain.

Whittington stared at the bloody stick in his hand. He tossed it away and staggered about in a daze looking for a way around the wall of debris that now included pieces of his car. His eyes lit on the rifle case lying amid broken glass and other shrapnel from the wreckage. The case was scuffed and dented, but intact. He knelt and opened it. The rifle was undamaged. He removed the gun and one of the boxes of shells and walked away leaving the flickering, smoking, sizzling mess behind him.

Lester was content to end the show with the big fireworks display, so he bent over to gather up his gear. He glanced up just in time to see Whittington disappear into the woods with a rifle. He stood for a second, staring open-mouthed in disbelief, then he took off running after him. He berated himself for trying to be a good guy. This was why it was better to just go ahead and kill some people.

Lester ran toward the gap in the trees where he'd seen the Professor go. He intended to catch him and put one in his head this time. The next thing he knew his feet went out from under him and he was swept through the air through no will of his own. When the motion arrested, he found himself snared in a tangle of slender nylon-coated cables. It was a bear snare. He'd stumbled into a dad-blasted poacher's snare.

The impact made Lester drop everything he was carrying and the cables trapped his hands against his torso. He and Fate were both carrying walkie talkies on their belts that were illegally-modified for long range use, but the device was just out of his reach. He strained against the metal cables until his hands were bleeding, but there was no way he could reach far enough to toggle the transmit button on the side of the radio.

He hung there in midair, bound, and looked up at the sky. At least the wind and rain had subsided slightly. The storm was moving on.

Gradually, he worked his hand down an inch more until with his middle finger, he was able to touch the squelch button on the top of the walkie talkie. He tapped out an S-O-S on it and waited. He hoped somehow Fate would hear it and come looking for him. He'd have to pass Hamilton's on the way, and he'd be extremely suspicious of Whittington, even wandering around on foot, so with any luck he'd intercept the Professor before he did any more harm. Lester smiled at the thought. No one in their right mind would want Fate coming after them.

Whittington was bushwhacking his way through the underbrush, hoping he would eventually find the road again. He thought he was going the right way, but it was taking too long. He must've gotten turned around.

It was difficult to stay oriented. He was wandering around, dazed by the prospect of exposure for his crimes, the fight with Henry, the car wreck, the explosion, the storm, and the surreal landscape. Things kept getting worse. And the bad things were happening with less and less recovery time in between. He felt hysterical. Then he thought he could make out several black blobs moving toward him in the darkness, converging on him from different directions. He was frightened that they might be bears, so he shot at them.

He was mistaken about the shadows, they weren't bears, but he'd have been even more terrified if he'd realized his wild potshots were summoning a 400 pound black bear who happened to be close enough to hear the distinctive pops of the silenced rifle. The bear loped off toward the sound, excited to see what Henry had made for dinner.

CHAPTER 40

When Professor Whittington saw the bear up close, he did the worst thing he could possibly do. He ran.

That virtually guaranteed that the bear would chase him, even though the fearsome creature wasn't at all interested in harming him, but was simply doing what he'd learned, for which he expected to receive a tasty pork treat.

Whittington sprinted along the most passable route he could discern and to his surprise and relief, burst out on the paved road. Hamilton's was just across the way. He continued toward it at his maximum speed. He glanced back over his shoulder and saw that the bear was still giving chase, not gaining on him, but following avidly.

Whittington didn't understand that the bear was looking for a wild hog, expecting Whittington to drop it. He dashed into the parking lot and zigzagged between the cars, jerking on the door handle of each one as he passed. The third one he tried was unlocked. It was Jill's new Mazda 323. He put one leg into the car, turned, and saw the bear closing in on him.

The sight was terrifying. Whittington threw himself the rest of the way into the car, and tried to slam the door, but the rifle he was carrying prevented it from closing. He dropped the gun on the ground and closed the door just seconds before the bear caught up with him. The bear raked the side of the car with his huge claws as a way of requesting his supper.

Whittington was trapped. The bear had him pinned inside the small car. The creature clawed and snarled ferociously as it climbed onto the hood and then the roof, looking for a way to reach the food it believed was inside.

It took less than a minute for the bear to force its claws through the rubber strip around the top of the driver's window and pry the glass out. Whittington scrambled across the console into the passenger seat. He opened the passenger door, intending to make a dash for the store, but the bear swatted at him with tremendous strength, unintentionally slamming it closed. Whittington sat inside, nearly paralyzed with fear.

The bear climbed down from the top of the car and set to work on the driver's door. Now that the glass was gone, the immensely strong and excited creature was able to get leverage with both paws on the window sill and rip the door off. Whittington screamed and clambered over the front seats into the back.

That was a really bad decision. He should have tried again to get out the passenger side. But he didn't realize his mistake until it was too late. Only after the bear had climbed into the front and was swatting at him between the seats, did he realize he was in the back seat of a two door car.

Henry lay on the ground with his right arm bleeding heavily. He had no idea what he'd been hit with. He assumed it was a bit of flying debris propelled up by the gale force winds. It was actually a bullet from one of the Professor's potshots.

It wasn't difficult for Leon to enlarge one of the rips in Henry's shirt and tear off a strip of fabric to make a tourniquet. He tied the piece of cloth around Henry's arm above the bulge of his bicep and got the bleeding slowed, but when Henry tried to stand he couldn't.

A moment later he felt Leon's hands grasp him under the arms. Henry still wasn't sure if he was hallucinating or if Leon was actually there. But someone lifted him with surprising strength and helped him to his feet. Then, with Leon half carrying him, he was able to make his way toward Hamilton's.

Phoebe looked out the window and a sudden flash of lightning lit the back yard. She couldn't believe her eyes. It was Henry and Leon! Leon was soaked and Henry looked a fright. What in the world had happened? And what in blue blazes was he doing out there? Phoebe grabbed a raincoat and ran for the back door. As soon as she went outside, before she could put the coat on, the wind jerked it out of her hand and carried it off into the storm.

She ran toward the two figures. When she got closer she saw that Henry was bleeding and could barely stand on his own. Leon was holding him upright. God have mercy. She had no idea what had happened, but whatever it was, it looked serious.

She went to Henry's other side and would have helped support him, but before she could, he pulled the rifle sling off over his head. He handed her the gun, the night vision headset, and the small plastic protective case containing the darts, and gasped, "Shoot!" and pointed out into the maelstrom.

"What?" she shouted, putting on the headgear and slipping a dart into the chamber.

"Go!" he shouted and shoved her hard toward the road.

She jogged around the side of the store and when she turned the corner, she saw a big bear destroying Jill's car.

An angry adult bear was a force of nature even more terrifying than the storm had been. Phoebe paused, watching the scene in amazement. The bear tore the driver's door off the car like he was opening a cardboard box. She made out the shape of someone scrambling over the front seat into the back.

A man's face suddenly appeared in the back window. He was trying to climb onto the small shelf behind the back seats. His shrieks could be heard over the howling of the wind.

Henry hobbled up behind her while she stared dumbly at the scene. He shouted at Phoebe again, "It's Whittington. For God's sake shoot!"

Phoebe lifted the rifle and aimed, "Which one?" she shouted. When Henry didn't answer her, she turned to find him on the ground with Leon kneeling over him.

The bear growled, the Professor let out a long hysterical scream, and Phoebe turned around and fired.

Immediately after making the shot she reloaded the gun.

The Professor's terrible screams went on for a few more seconds, but the drug quickly took effect and the bear grew sluggish, wobbly, then the big fellow fell out of the driver's seat through the opening made by the missing door and lay on the ground. When the bear went down, Whittington scrambled into the front seat, presumably to attempt a getaway. The whole side of his body was exposed by the missing door. Phoebe put her next shot into his thigh.

She reloaded the rifle with the last dart and would've put another one into his chest just for good measure, but Leon ran to the Professor and jerked the dart out of his leg. Whittington's mouth dropped open, his head rolled back, and he fell sideways out of the car, landing beside the paralyzed bear.

That was an image Phoebe would never forget. But Leon dragged the inert Professor away from the bear and whipped his belt off and used it as a tourniquet around the Professor's upper thigh.

Phoebe stomped over to where Leon knelt. "What're ye doin that for?" she shouted.

"Bear juice'll kill him," Leon shouted back. "It's too much."

"Like I *said*," Phoebe repeated, "What ye doin *that* for?"

Leon tightened the belt to his satisfaction, then ran into the store to get Doc.

Doc was still in the café assembling a deluxe cold dinner for himself and the ladies, blissfully unaware of the drama being played out in the parking lot. He'd made elaborate sandwiches and poured them glasses of milk, but he was having trouble finding plates and a tray.

Leon burst through the door looking like the survivor of a shipwreck and called, "Doc, will you come out here and take a look at that Professor fellow? Phoebe's shot him with Henry's bear juice. I got the dart out as quick as I could, but I don't know how much of it he got in him. Maybe too much."

"Don't worry Leon," Doc said calmly, without interrupting his search of the cabinets over the sink, "People like him always make it."

Phoebe gave the Professor an extremely cursory examination, using the toe of her boot rather more strongly than necessary to move him to and fro, and not really caring what she found. She went to tend to Henry.

There was no point in calling 911 or trying to drive Henry to the hospital because of all the trees in the road. And there was no way a helicopter could make it in this wind. So she and Doc worked on Henry. Then she took some bandages and tape over to where the Professor lay.

They'd left him lying on the ground with the bear. He started to come around while Phoebe was using gauze and tape to bind his ankles. She kicked him over on to his side and tied his wrists and then she bound his wrists and ankles together behind his back. She was finishing up when Fate arrived on the scene. He'd heard Lester's emergency transmission and come looking for him.

Fate put the tip of his rifle against the Professor's chest and used it like a stick to hold him in place. In the other hand he held a chainsaw. He looked at Phoebe and said, "Ya'll kin go on inside now and get dry. I'll take care of this for ye."

"Thanks Fate," Phoebe said. "But I'm not sure if he should go to the hospital first or to the cops."

"I know right where he needs to go," said Fate, in a tone that would've curdled Whittington's blood if he hadn't been doped out of his mind.

Phoebe was torn. Part of her wanted to let Fate dispose of the rascal. She had no doubt he'd do so in a thoroughly professional manner that would never come back on any of them. She was still mulling over Fate's offer when she was startled to hear Henry's voice behind her.

"That's a *mighty* attractive offer, sir. *Mighty* attractive," Henry said, "But the fool ruined a perfectly good hat of mine, so, if it's all the same to you, I'd like to turn him over to the law enforcement rangers."

Fate looked at Henry, smiled slightly, and nodded. He moved the barrel of his gun away from Whittington's chest and said, "If ye change yer mind … ."

Whittington's eyes opened, but he still didn't have much motor coordination. He moaned and thrashed half-heartedly at his restraints. Fate leaned over into the man's face and gave him a look that silenced him. Then he dangled the chainsaw where Whittington could see it. Whittington's eye grew wide.

"Aw, Fate there's no need to waste gas with the saw," Leon teased, "Phoebe's got some scalpels."

Whittington screamed like a little girl.

Leon half-carried Henry into the store. He sat him at a table in the café and asked Jill to bring him something hot to drink. Moments later Phoebe plopped down beside Henry.

They all looked like road kill.

"Who'd ye shoot first?" asked Henry.

"The bear."

Henry nodded, "Good choice."

"Do you need to do anything to him?"

"Nah, when he wakes up, he'll run off and, after the awful way you've treated him, I can personally guarantee that he'll never come back to this area again.

"Wonder what's the best way to get the insurance to pay for the damage to Jill's car? Should she claim human or animal damage?"

"Why not both?" said Henry.

Phoebe looked at him, trying to really see him this time. He was a wreck. "Do you get tore up like this often?"

"Yeah," he said, sighing. "I guess I'm lucky I know a good nurse."

They both laughed and Phoebe leaned forward to hug him. He winced, thought about asking her for a rain check on the hug, then changed his mind and hugged her back with the arm that had a bullet in it, saying "Owwww!"

CHAPTER 41

It was spring by the time the authorities got things sorted out well enough to schedule a press conference about the discovery of the new drug.

Ivy had made a full recovery from her ordeal. She'd always have a small scar at her temple, but she didn't mind. It reminded her of how tough she was and how every achievement came at a price. Henry's arm healed well, attended to assiduously by Phoebe. Henry had good government insurance so Waneeta made sure Appalachian Healthcare got paid for services rendered.

Phoebe and Henry had a date to attend the ceremony honoring Ivy at Twin Creeks. The event was drawing major media attention. Ivy was going to sign the official document with the National Park Service confirming the location of her discovery, thereby guaranteeing the park would receive half of the proceeds from the commercialization of the substance produced by the new species of slime mold she'd found.

So far only a couple of people knew it, but Ivy had named the medicine *jillleoncillin* in honor of Jill and Leon's crucial interventions to rescue her and her specimens and she'd named the myxo *Physarum polycephalum smokus phoebehenrii* to thank her other benefactors. Pharmaceutical analysts on Wall Street were predicting that the new antibiotic would be worth tens, if not hundreds, of millions of dollars. So the park's share was a lot of money. Phoebe hoped some of that would eventually trickle down into a raise for Henry and some additional full-time positions in wildlife management, but she knew that was unlikely since Henry and his boss were getting along even worse than usual in the aftermath of the brouhaha.

Park Superintendent Fielding read Henry the riot act about his unauthorized use of a motor vehicle in the park. And he went purple in the face when berating him for allowing a National Park Service animal tranquilizer rifle to be operated by unauthorized personnel, and even worse, for advocating the use of said rifle on a human being!

Henry was also severely admonished about involving himself in events outside the boundary of the national park. But after a comprehensive tongue-lashing, Superintendent Fielding grudgingly mumbled that he'd decided not to fire Henry. He wasn't honest enough to admit that it was because without Henry's so-called inappropriate activities, the park would've had no share in the profits from Ivy's discovery.

Henry endured the dressing down with as much equanimity as he could muster. He even kept a straight face during Fielding's rants about the importance of following the rules, setting a good example, and maintaining the public's trust in government servants.

When he was sure his boss was finished, Henry reached into the breast pocket of his uniform shirt and took out the brass key stamped *GSM-147* and set it carefully on the Superintendent's desk. He'd had a chance to talk to Ivy about the cabin and she'd told him it was Fielding's secret love nest. She knew she was only one of several women who'd been given keys. She'd made it clear that she had no interest in his advances, but Fielding urged her to keep the key in case of emergency, to give himself plausible deniability.

Next, he set the nickel Sequoia cone hatband ornament beside it. Henry waited for Fielding to grasp the significance of the two items, then, when he saw the Superintendent's eyes widen, he left the office without saying a single word.

The University of Tennessee was scrambling to handle their own debacle quietly, behind the scenes. First, they had to decide how to deal with a young graduate student who'd made a discovery of major significance to both science and medicine, and simultaneously lost her major professor, and nearly her life, under circumstances that were extremely awkward to say the least.

The University was trapped between a rock and a hard place. They wanted to minimize the scandal but were also desperate to horn in on the media storm surrounding Ivy. The kid was already the youngest person to make the cover of *Fungi* magazine.

The President, Chancellor, and Dean of the Botany Department met with Ivy to assure her that she would be getting an ethical and cooperative new major professor and that she would be awarded her doctorate on an expedited schedule if she made any gesture whatsoever toward completing the requirements.

A worldwide bidding war broke out among the pharmaceutical conglomerates, but Ivy was talking to Weleda, trying to convince them to function as her primary agent so the new antibiotic would be made available as naturally and cheaply as possible. Tests by scientists confirmed that the compound was indeed effective for treating brain infections that had previously been fatal.

As a way of paying back the people who saved her life and protected her discovery, Ivy had already signed the paperwork to establish a foundation for rural healthcare. The Foundation would begin by building a combination childcare, eldercare, hospice, and special needs respite facility for the town of White Oak.

She asked Phoebe, Doc, Jill, Leon, and Henry to serve on the Board of Directors.

Leon promised Ivy that when she was feeling up to it, he'd show her more places with distinctive micro-climates like the one where she'd made her discovery. His grandmaw had shown him several such places on their herb gathering trips.

Because Ivy, Phoebe, Waneeta, and Jill wore Jill's colorful creations at all the media events, Jill's business exploded. Her upgrades of traditional Appalachian rags were featured in magazines from *Altered Couture* to *Vogue*.

Cloud Forest's boutique was selling out of her coats as fast as she could make them and custom orders were coming in at a dizzying rate via Etsy.com. The business needed an official name so, *Goodwill Jill* became *Queenagers* with a sideline for younger people called *Ragamuffin*.

The jobs created by the expansion of Jill's business would give a nice boost to the local economy. And it was great news for the regulars at the café, too, because Jill wouldn't have time for them anymore. They appreciated her years of effort on their behalf, but the truth was she wasn't much of a chef. They were hoping she'd hire someone with real talent, but nobody had the courage or bad manners to suggest this to her directly. Instead, they put out a request via the local gossips for a good cook to put in an application.

Professor Whittington was residing in a jail cell in the Riverbend Maximum Security Institution in Nashville. In solitary confinement for his own safety, he believed himself to be more secure in prison than he would've been on the outside. He'd have felt a lot less secure if he'd realized how far Lester and Fate's network extended.

After Ivy signed the deal with the park, there was a gala reception benefiting Appalachian Bear Rescue. Henry and Phoebe had arrived together, which was sure to start a lot of tongues wagging. As they made their way toward the buffet table they passed Waneeta and Professor Van Landingham standing together, deep in conversation. Waneeta had a hand on the Frog Whisperer's arm and was obviously charming the socks off him.

When Waneeta saw Phoebe and Henry, she winked and gestured at them with a cute little four-fingered wave that Phoebe interpreted for Henry, "It looks like we have a go for husband number four."

As Phoebe reached for a cookie she heard Waneeta say, "Walter, honey, will you do the chorus frog again? I just love that one."

ACKNOWLEDGMENTS

This book could never have been written without a lot of help. I'm especially grateful for the assistance of Dave DeBruicker. Many thanks also to friends who read and commented on drafts of the manuscript – Mary Benami, Wendy Welch, Martha Eddington, Sandy Johanson, Fran Hoffman, Jill Draper, Yvonne Loveday, Elise Jourdan (Momma), and the amazing Richard McWhorter.

Shout out to Jill Kerttula who has been such a blessing in my life, making custom coats that give me courage to cope with large speaking engagements. www.Jill2day.com

Admiration, respect, and gratitude go out to Kim DeLozier, Rick Varner, and Dan Nolfi, brave wildlife rangers who struggle to protect park visitors and critters from each other 24/7/365 without ever breaking any rules.

Deep gratitude to Dr. R. Wayne Van Devender who is a real Frog Whisperer and one of the most impressive teachers I've ever had the privilege to meet. Thanks also to Dr. Sydney Everhart, the real myxomycete expert who unintentionally inspired this book by scampering around in the treetops and startling the heck out of me.

And thanks to several friends who appear as characters in this book but refused to allow me to identify them. You all know who each other are.

ABOUT THE AUTHOR

A former U.S. Senate Counsel to the Committee on Environment and Public Works and the Committee on Governmental Affairs, Carolyn Jourdan has degrees from the University of Tennessee in Biomedical Engineering and Law.

Carolyn lives on the family farm in Strawberry Plains, Tennessee, with many stray animals.

Her first book, **Heart in the Right Place**, is a *Wall Street Journal* bestselling comical memoir. It's the true story of a spoiled, high-powered Senate lawyer (Carolyn) who gives up a glamorous life in Washington and comes back home to the Smoky Mountains to work as an inept receptionist in her father's rural medical office. It was voted the #1 Nonfiction Pick in the Nation, a Best Book of the Year, a Best Book Club Book of the Year, and a Most Fun Book Ever. It was also selected as *Family Circle* magazine's first ever Book of the Month and awarded the *Elle* magazine Readers Prize.

Her second book, **Medicine Men: Extreme Appalachian Doctoring**, is also a bestseller. It's a collection of true stories describing the most memorable moments from the lives of a dozen physicians who practiced alone in the rural Southern Appalachian Highlands from the 1930's to 2005.

She is also the co-author of the *Bear in the Back Seat: Adventures of a Wildlife Ranger in the Great Smoky Mountains National Park* series.

For updates, visit Carolyn's website at www.CarolynJourdan.com

Be a Friend of Carolyn's personal Facebook page at www.Facebook.com/CarolynJourdan or Like her public page at www.Facebook.com/CarolynJourdanAuthor

CPSIA information can be obtained
at www.ICGtesting.com
Printed in the USA
LVHW02s0216290618
582270LV00026B/1017/P